HOOD WITCHES

NIKKI BROWN

DISCLAIMER

This book is not like other works I've written. It is a paranormal/fantasy novella. The characters will use magic, spells and other fictional aspects to make certain things happen. If you are not into that kind of thing. Stop reading here!!!!! Thank you for your support!

"That's my song!" Shya yelled over the sounds of *Trip by Ella Mai,* as it blared through the speakers of Club Met. Throwing her hands in the air she wound her perfectly sculpted hips in a circle as she sang along with every word. The short black dress that she had on left nothing to the imagination, and the more she wound her hips the more of a show she began putting on for the other patrons whose attention she had gained.

Jalan, Shya's sister, leaned back against the bar as she watched her younger sister have the time of her life. She smiled as Shya turned her way and motioned for her to join her on the dance floor. Any other time, Jalan would have been more than happy to join her sister in a dance off, but tonight she was on a mission and didn't want to be shied away from the goal at hand.

Earlier today, Jalan went through her boyfriend of two years emails and found out that not only was he cheating on her again, but he was doing it right under her nose and with a girl she claimed as her friend. Feeling the need to catch him in the act, Jalan planned a night out with her sister at the very club that Channing, her boyfriend was planning to meet up with Zeta at.

"Jalan what's wrong with you? I didn't come out to party by myself. Don't make me cast a spell and make your hips do that thing like last time." Shya made her way back over to where her sister was in an attempt to get her to lighten her spirits.

Shya was the jokester of the two sisters. She had an aura about her that made you want to be around her. Yet her playful banter and her magical abilities didn't always mix, Jalan had been on the receiving end of her wild spells once or twice. Whereas Shya loved to indulge in a sassy spell here and there, Jalan saved her talents for her potions and magic oils, unless her sister forced her to do so.

"If you do that Shya, I promise I will make you bald in front of all of these people." Jalan pointed at her and Shya held her hands up in surrender. The two sisters shared a laugh right as something caught Jalan's eye and commanded her attention.

Shya, sensing that something was wrong with her sister, followed her eyes and watched as her sister's boyfriend grinded all on her sister's friend. Shya knew there was something that she didn't like about Zeta, but Jalan always begged her to give her a chance.

Shya's eyes narrowed instantly and her fist balled. She raised one foot and was headed in that direction when Jalan grabbed her arm and pulled her back. This wasn't the first time that she had been blindsided by her sister on a mission to find her cheating boyfriend. Shya didn't understand why her sister put up with Channing's mess.

As far as Shya was concerned, they both could have any man that they wanted. With skin the color of warm vanilla, almond shaped eyes and medium sized lips, the sisters shared their mothers' dark curly hair and slim thick shape. The sisters were identical to each other, even with Jalan being two years Shya's senior. Outside of Shya's honey colored eyes you could barely tell them apart at times.

"That's why you brought me all the way out here ain't it?" Shya fussed, jerking away from her sister. Her arms crossed across her chest as she put more weight on one foot than she did the other causing her thick hips to stick out more than normal.

Her light brown eyes had taken on a gray color, as they normally did when she was upset, and Jalan could feel the cussing that she was about to receive from Shya for bringing her along once again to chase her no count boyfriend.

"Shya just let it go, I just needed to see the shit for myself."

"No fuck that!" the fair skinned beauty boasted as she stared her sister down. "You drug me all the way out here, fucked up my night, and you think you ain't gone let me have some fun with this?" Shya tugged at the little black dress as she looked up to the sky thinking of the perfect spell to cast on the unfaithful bastard that her sister was head over heels in love with.

"Shya let's just go," Jalan whispered into deaf ears. She began shaking her head as a wicked smile spread across Shya's face.

In that moment Jalan was regretting pulling her sister into her mess. She knew what a hot head Shya could be at times like this. She worried about her little sister because she was quite crafty with her words and spells and she hadn't even gotten her full powers yet.

"Here we go."

"No, I got it!" Jalan yelled in an attempt to stop Shya. She knew that if she cast the spell it wouldn't be as bad as her sister's.

Shya gave her sister an evil look, she knew exactly what she was doing. All she wanted to do was have some fun seeing as though her night had been ruined by her sister's bullshit. Now she was being held back from that. Shya was definitely gonna make Jalan pay for that so she may as well get ready for it.

"Go on with your weak spell." Shya rolled her eyes and prepared the perfect spell just in case Jalan froze up as she normally did.

> *"I've told you once,*
> *I've told you twice,*
> *fucking with me is nothing nice.*
> *To my warning you did not take heed,*
> *now everyone must see you bleed!"*

Jalan tucked her hair behind her left ear, an indicator that her spell was done and ready to be cast.

The Hood sisters stood back and watched as the snow-white calf length Capri pants that Zeta donned slowly began to turn firetruck engine red.

"Oh my god bitch! You don't know how to put on a tampon? You ol' nasty ass!" Shya cupped her hands around her mouth and yelled as loud as she could causing the small crowd that had surrounded them to look down at Zeta's white jeans.

Zeta was so embarrassed that she took off towards the bathroom. Her period had just gone off, so she was sure that it was safe to wear the white pants out for her date with Channing. She had been waiting on her chance to get a piece of him since her friend Jalan bragged about how good he was in bed every chance she got.

Now that she finally had her chance, she was standing in the bathroom wondering why she was leaking blood like a faucet. She covered her face with her hands and silently cried to herself. He would never look at her the same.

Bursting out of the bathroom, Zeta made a beeline for the door. She was thanking herself for suggesting they meet up a couple towns over, to make sure that her friend didn't see her out and about with her man. Deep down in her heart, Zeta envied Jalan, from the way she looked to the way she carried herself.

Jalan was everything that Zeta wanted to be, but she was too selfish and self-centered to ever match up to the gorgeous Jalan. On her way out the door she could have sworn she saw Jalan in the distance, but she didn't stop to make sure. She got out of there as fast as she could.

"Zeta! Zeta! Zeta!" Channing yelled as he chased after his girlfriend's best friend.

"You let him off too easy," Shya fussed at her sister.

Shya had never been in love. The thought aggravated her at times because she knew that the first man she would ever love would have to be sacrificed, so she was in no hurry to do so. That part of witchery was the only part that Shyla hated. Why couldn't she just be happy, cast spells and live her life how she wanted? Why did she have to sacrifice a man that she would grow to have feelings for in order to gain her full powers and live happily ever after?

"You will never understand until you're in my shoes," Jalan said as she watched the man that she thought she loved run out after another woman.

"It's your fault he's like this," Shya reminded her sister. It was because of her own deceitful actions against witchery that Channing acts the way he does anyway.

Jalan rolled her eyes right before she waved her sister off. The two had had this argument before. Being two years older than her sister, Jalan had already been through the worse part of their culture.

Thinking that she was outsmarting the system, Jalan fell in love with two men, she wanted to make sure that she had a choice for the Love Ritual. The day of her 21st birthday she made a choice, she chose to sacrifice Sarif who truly did love her, but what she didn't know was that Channing wasn't the man she thought he was.

By the time she realized that she had made a mistake it was too late. Not wanting to hear the *I told you so* from her mother, Jalan cast a spell to make Channing love her. Knowing that was against the rules she did it anyway, any consequence was better than hearing her mother chastise her about not being a good witch, or so she thought.

"Do you have to keep bringing that up?"

"I'm sorry Jalan but you knew if you used your powers to try and make a man love you that the spell would reverse, and he would do the opposite." Shya gave her sister a sympathetic look. She loved her sister dearly, but she hated that she kept putting herself out there for a man that she knew would never be what she wanted or needed. It wasn't possible, and she made sure of that.

"If I would have known the severity of the consequences then I wouldn't have done it Shya."

Part of that was true but she was so desperate for that forever type of love that she would do just about anything, including taking her lying piece of shit boyfriend back after he cheated on her for the thousandth time. Shya knew that and that's why she tried her best to keep her sister grounded.

"Look, let's just have a good time. No need in wasting a good night. You saw what you needed to see, now unless you want to go fuck them both up, I'm not about to waste a damn good dress." Shya put her hands on her hips.

Even though Jalan was in no mood to party, she knew that she would never hear the end of it if she didn't show her sister a good time. Her heart was breaking in a million pieces and she just wanted someone to mend it, someone who wouldn't mend it just to break it again.

$\mathscr{H}$ 2 $\mathscr{H}$

"Yo if that bitch come back in this section, I swear I'mma make her wish she never had," Shiloh said to his brother over the music.

The night wasn't going as planned. The two brothers had every intention on coming out and enjoying themselves tonight, but the busted women who kept finding their way into their VIP section was turning this night into a bust.

"Chill nigga damn, with yo hostile ass." Ziloh's eyes scanned the club in search of his next target. Ziloh was a bit of a lady's man and never missed a chance to invade a woman's personal space. He promised himself that he would never fall in love with another woman after losing the love of his life just three years ago.

He had vowed to keep everyone at arm's length, and offer up one thing, good dick. That came with ease. Looking over at his brother who wore a mug as the girl he warned not to come back over to his section sauntered her way right back in. He shook his head because he knew right then that this was about to go left and quick.

"What the fuck I just tell you hoe?" Shiloh said turning up the bottle of Hennessy that he had in his hands. The look that he gave her would have sent anybody else packing, but this girl wasn't catching any of the hints that Shiloh was throwing at her.

"I'm just trying to party, you know no strings attached. I'm Tanala by the way." The girl gave Shiloh a toothless grin and that took him over the edge. Slowly placing the bottle on the table, he looked her up and down.

Nothing about the girl was appealing to Shiloh. Her bright yellow skin was covered in freckles, and not the cute ones but the ones that had no purpose. Her eyes were too far apart which made her nose stick out more than it should. Her thin lips matched the awkwardness of her face. She was skinny, not an ounce of fat on her but her confidence was through the roof. But even that couldn't help her.

Shiloh's eyes traveled from her eyes down to the plastic baby doll shoes she had on her feet. Making his way back up to her face she had the nerve to run her tongue along her bottom lip.

"Oh shit!" Ziloh said and placed his fist over his mouth to keep from laughing. He knew what was about to happen before his brother grabbed his dick.

"Omg god!" the girl screamed as her poorly made synthetic wig flew off her head and across the dance floor where the party goers took turns stepping on it as they never missed a beat.

Shiloh and Ziloh shared a look before they both burst out laughing. Ziloh shook his head at his brother before he looked down at the girl trying to catch her wig that kept getting away from her.

"Yo nigga chill out," Ziloh barely got out from laughing.

"Nah, maybe that shit will keep her busy." He joined in on the laughter. That wasn't the first time that Shiloh used his powers to get rid of an unwanted guest and it wouldn't be the last. That was about the only time that he embraced his warlock-hood, unlike his brother who relished in witchcraft.

"What the fuck is that?" a beautiful yet powerful voice could be heard from the dance floor of club Met.

The voice carried into Shiloh's heart and pulled him out of his seat. Before he knew it, he was standing up and searching for the mouth the melodic tune came from. His eyes zoomed back and forth across the dance floor until they fell on the girl chasing her wig and the beauty who was yelling about what was flying around on the floor.

Having enough of the charades, Shiloh grabbed his dick again and the wig stopped in its tracks. Tanala bent down to pick up the cheap wig that she spent the little child support she gets on, but not before screaming a few obscenities to the beauty who had Shiloh's full attention.

It was something about her smooth, vanilla colored skin and her funny looking eyes that had Shiloh in a trance. The way her thick lips poked out indicating that she was pissed off had Shiloh imagining them wrapped around his dick while he gripped her hair and guided her up and down his shaft.

"Damn," he mumbled under his breath while he made his way to where the action was going down. He could hear his brother calling his name, but he ignored him. He had more pressing things to deal with at the present moment.

"Bitch I don't know who you think you are, but you got the right one!" Talana yelled at the beautiful girl.

The closer Shiloh got to Shya the more he was intrigued with her. She didn't argue back with the ghetto girl she just gave her look that said she wasn't to be messed with.

"Check this out little girl." Jalan walked into view and she was just as equally beautiful as Shya. They were both on the short side barely reaching 5'5", Shy had more hips and butt than Jalan, but she wasn't lacking either. They could have passed as twins if it weren't for the fact that Shya's eyes did the color change where as Jalan's didn't.

Ziloh had just joined the fun and made his way over to where his brother was standing just staring at Shya. Ziloh had never seen his brother that intrigued by a woman before, it was like she had him in some kind of trance.

Shiloh was so enthralled with the woman in front of him that he never realized that his brother was present until he touched his shoulder.

"Bruh you good?" Ziloh asked drawing attention from Shya and Jalan.

When Shya and Shiloh's eyes met it was like magic happening in the midst of all of the drama that was unfolding in front of them. Neither of them said anything, they just stared at each other.

Out of habit, Shya tucked her hair behind her ears and folded her arms across her chest, causing her breast to spill out of the top of the small black dress. Shiloh's eyes went right to where the action was taking place, drawing a lip smack from Shya.

"Can I help you with something?" a smirk slowly graced her face causing one to appear on Shiloh's. He was normally a no-nonsense kind of guy but being in this beauty's presence was bringing something out of him that he couldn't control, and to be honest, he didn't want to.

"So, this is the kind of bitches you like huh? You like them stuck up hoes that act like they shit don't stank? That's why you was acting like a bitch," Tanala said with her wig still in her hands. She was just trying to find her a new sponsor for the night, her rent was due, and she needed to bag a baller until she got her bills caught up. Her baby daddy had just got locked up, so he wasn't in the position to help her.

She just knew she had bagged a baller in the VIP until he opened his mouth and dissed her. She still didn't give up and planned to keep working him until she wore him down. That was until he saw the little freaky eyed bitch and any chances of her slipping in his bed tonight diminished the second their eyes connected.

"Dead ass, they gone find you floating up the river if you don't get the fuck out of my face. I don't know who you think I am, but a nigga's dick got standards and I wouldn't fuck yo nasty looking ass if I was paid to do so. Now it's in your best interest to get the fuck out of my face before I forget how my mama raised me." Shiloh's voice was even and calm. He didn't feel the need to raise his voice or talk loud, his presence was enough.

Tanala didn't want to keep trying her luck, she was sure she would see him around again and planned to work her magic. Hopefully next time she would be able to splurge on a better outfit and shoes. She looked down at her wig that was still in her hand and rolled her eyes at the woman that she was blaming for messing up her night. Making sure to leave as dramatically as possible she made sure to connect with Shya's shoulder as she left.

"That was mean not nice at all.
Fall to your knees, to the door you must crawl!"

Shya turned her head and tucked her hair behind her right ear, right before Tanala took a dive to the floor. Shya looked on as the girl tried her best to get up off the floor to no avail. A small giggle left Shya's and Jalan's lips as they watched the girl crawl to the door to get out while everyone in her path laughed.

"Excuse me fellas, we have to be going," Jalan said grabbing Shya's arm and pulling her out of the little circle the group had formed. Shya's last spell was a little too close for Jalan's liking. The last thing that she needed was for someone in this town to see them using witchcraft, and it would cause a whole other issue that the sisters have had to deal with in the past.

"Wait!" Shiloh yelled out almost desperately. The sisters stopped in their tracks and turned toward the handsome gentlemen. It was then that Jalan got a really good look at the man that was standing with him.

Unable to stop the smile that graced her face, she burst into a full-fledged giggle that quickly went away when her reality hit her in the face and she saw Channing, who was oblivious that she was even there still, at the bar entertaining another woman. She shook her head and turned around to leave.

Shya saw exactly what her sister saw, she was pissed and tired of him treating her sister that way. Walking closer to where he was and away from the handsome duo, she narrowed her eyes at him.

"You hurt my sister,
you hurt her bad,
you made her cry,
you made her sad.
You never loved her, no not at all.
Now it's time to make you small."

Tucking her hair behind her right ear she smiled as she watched him grab himself and shook his leg like something was wrong. He looked down at his pants and his eyebrows furrowed as a slow and controlled smile appeared on Shya's face. When he excused himself from the lady he was entertaining, she knew her job was done.

Satisfied with her actions, she headed towards the door to find her sister. Right when she reached the door someone grabbed her arm. Shya snapped her head around and came face to face with the man that had captured her attention and weirdly a small piece of her heart in merely minutes.

"I need you see you again," he said.

"If you *need* to see me then you'll find a way to see me." Shya smiled and so did Shiloh. He was definitely feeling her vibe and wanted to make sure that he was in her presence and soon.

"At least tell me your name, I'm Shiloh."

"Shya, Shya Hood." With that Shya removed her hand from the stranger's and headed to find her sister. She was sure that the handsome stranger would plague her thoughts all night.

❄ 3 ❄

I t was past three in the morning and Channing was making his way from the club. He had every intention of going home with the beauty that he had met but something weird was going on below his waist and to save himself the embarrassment he just went home. Channing had never had that issue, he was experiencing extreme shrinkage and his dick wouldn't get hard for nothing. He made a mental note to call his doctor first thing Monday morning.

Walking in the house, it felt quieter than normal. He just knew that Jalan was gonna be up waiting for him so she could argue, but to his surprise she wasn't. Her car was outside, so he knew s he was there so why she wasn't up waiting was baffling to him.

Heading through the house to search for her, he walked into their bedroom and it was empty. Alarm set in as he moved throughout the house in search of the woman that he took for granted on the regular.

"Jalan? Where you at baby?" he called out as he headed upstairs to the attic. When he opened the door, there she sat in a rocking chair just looking out the window. Her head slowly turned towards Channing's direction as she focused in on his appearance.

"What's up?" was all she offered. Channing wasn't feeling the disconnect that he was feeling right now so he walked in her direction with his arms spread wide causing Jalan to laugh. "Nah playa, I'm good."

Turning her head back to look out the window the two got lost in an uncomfortable silence, neither of them said anything. Jalan because she knew if she did that things would get ugly and she was starting to realize that she would never be able to correct the mistake she made years ago. Tired of being hurt she knew that this thing she had with Channing was way past gone and she was tired of fighting.

"Well I'm gonna go shower." Channing may as well have been talking to himself because Jalan's thoughts were on anything but him right now. The smile that graced her face had Channing confused and wondering what was going on with her.

Channing couldn't explain his change in attitude for Jalan, when they first met, he just knew that she would be everything that he had prayed for in a woman. He still had his flaws, but he knew that he could change for her. Then it was like one night he went to bed and when he woke up everything that he felt for her was gone.

She was no longer a woman that he desired but just someone to pass the time until the *right woman* came along. Channing racked his brain trying to figure out where his feelings for Jalan went but he chalked it up as her not being the one. So, his search for the one increased and that's where he found himself with Zeta.

Zeta was outgoing and fun, she didn't worry so much about what people thought and she didn't feel the need to control things. She let him be the man. With Jalan, he felt like he had to be someone he wasn't. She had always acted as if she was better than him and that's the reason he remained shut off from her.

What he didn't know was that Jalan had to put on a front because she didn't want people to know about her witchery. She couldn't do certain things and she tried to keep herself from getting too angry to where she would lash out like she's done before. So, her being reserved and more to herself was for his safety, he just didn't know it.

"Cool!" Jalan offered and then looked down at her phone at a text from her sister, telling her to play it cool and that he was not worth the energy. Jalan was trying so hard to listen to her baby sister. The task was indeed hard, but she planned to tough it out.

"Is everything okay?" Channing asked still staring at a very different Jalan, she was normally clingy and suffocating but not today.

"Yep! Have a good night."

"You not coming to bed?" Channing asked incredulously.

"Nah!" she shook her head indicating that what he heard was correct. He opened his mouth to say something right before he closed it back. He was at a loss for words and that was a first. After Channing disappeared out of the attic, Jalan threw her head back and cried.

This had been her routine for the entire two years of their relationship, even more when she chose to let him live over Sarif. She felt like this was her Karma for trying to outsmart witchery. She should have just followed the rules and she wouldn't be in this mess.

Jalan made herself a promise, she would make sure that her sister did everything that she was supposed to do so that she never ended up like her. She never wanted her sister to feel the way that she was feeling.

Closing her eyes, Jalan took in a deep breath and released it as slow as she could.

"Tomorrow is a new day and I will be a new woman," she chanted to herself over and over until sleep consumed her. Meet the new Jalan Hood!

4

October first had come and gone, and Shiloh dreaded each day that passed. He knew what was to come at the end of the month and to say he wasn't looking forward to it was an understatement. It didn't help that his brother reminded him of it constantly, like now.

"Bruh yo it's easy, find a chick you dig make the hoe fall in love and sacrifice her ass. Simple as that nigga," Ziloh shrugged his shoulders. Shiloh gave him a look that warned him to stop talking but it was ignored as he continued to try and down play the Love Ritual that Shiloh was trying his hardest not to think about.

Deep down, Ziloh knew what he was saying wasn't true. Sacrificing someone that you had grown accustomed to and had developed feelings for wasn't the walk in the park he described. He was trying to make the situation as easy for his brother as possible.

Ziloh didn't want his brother to feel what he felt, so he tried to put it in his head that it wasn't anything, just something that had to be done. He still had nightmares about Jerica often, which is why he hardly slept.

"Ziloh that shit might be easy for you, but I don't wanna do that shit." He threw his hands up in the air. "Who in the fuck wants to get close to a bitch just to kill her?"

The harshness of Shiloh's words punched Ziloh in the gut, but as normal he played it off with his witty and silly banter. He often masked his feelings with his sarcastic jokes, and for the most part it worked because no one knew that he was silently still mourning the death of his first love.

"You thinking too much into it brother. You don't have to love her. You just have to make her love you." Ziloh smiled and buried his hands deep into his pockets. He was antagonizing his brother on purpose, something that he took pleasure in from time to time.

"And that takes time, wasted time." Shiloh sighed heavily as he threw his head in his hands. He didn't think that this would bother him as much as it did and meeting the beauty from the club only made that worse.

His thoughts switched to her as his brother kept going on and on about the sacrifice that he would have to make at the end of the month. As bad as he wanted to see her and be in her presence, he knew that he couldn't. It was something about her, and he knew that if given the chance he could fall for her easily.

Without even a conversation he knew that the two could be amazing together. Now was just bad ass timing. Shaking his head, he turned his attention back to his brother.

"Well you really ain't got a choice. It's either that or you're cast down into damnation." Ziloh raised his eyebrow, "I'm sure you don't want that. The bitches down there are burnt as fuck!" His face was neutral, not showing one hint of humor in it and that caused Shiloh to laugh for the first time today. "You laughing, but I'm dead ass nigga."

"That's the fucking problem!" Shiloh shook his head and then stood up from where he was sitting and headed to the bathroom. Staring into the mirror he looked at himself and wondered if he would be able to do what was being asked of him. Shiloh and Ziloh ran one of the most lucrative drug empires that the world has ever seen so it was crazy to him that he was having so much trouble with this. The brothers had killed before without so much as an after thought but those people deserved it. An innocent was just that, innocent, but this had to be done and he knew it. "Get your shit together nigga," he coached himself.

After taking a piss and washing his hands he joined his brother who had taken his place on the couch in front of the Xbox.

"This muthafucka cheating!" Ziloh yelled as he brushed his hands down his shirt and then automatically the game score shot up to put him on top.

"Nigga you using magic to fucking beat a game, and you talking about them cheating?" Shiloh laughed at his brother.

"Shit, I'm just trying to even the score." With a shrug of the shoulders, he continued to move his fingers around the game controller as he attempted to outsmart Madden. "What we got today?" Ziloh asked not really paying attention to anything outside the game.

"I got a text from Eevie and she said they were out on the southside, so I know that she's coming through. Jax on his way with Channing," Shiloh said looking at his phone. "Fuck I didn't realize that it was so late, I ain't gone have time to cook the dope."

"Why the fuck would you cook the dope nigga?" Ziloh pressed pause on the game. It pissed him off that Shiloh was so shy with his powers until someone pissed him off. The way he saw it, the two were blessed and chosen, which is why he understood that the Love Ritual was something that had to be done. It was their way of giving back to the universe for making them special.

Ziloh stood up and stretched his hands over his head and then shook his head at his brother. Grabbing his dick pre-bagged coke appeared on the table in front of where Shiloh was standing. He brushed his hands down the front of his shirt a few times and pounds of weed appeared to the left of the coke.

"Lazy ass nigga." Shiloh rubbed his hands across his head and the pills that were going to the southside appeared at Ziloh's feet causing Shiloh to chuckle.

"You an asshole," Ziloh mumbled as he lifted his hand and watched the pills follow it. He waved his hands and the pills flew over to where the rest of the drugs were. "There, everything ready."

"We still gotta separate it. Damn you just don't believe in getting ya hands dirty do you nigga?" Shiloh fussed and Ziloh said something under his breath before he grabbed his dick again and everything was separated and ready to go.

"No matter how you think of it brother, we were blessed with a gift and I plan to use it to the best of my abilities. You need to get onboard." Ziloh gave his brother a knowing look.

"Yeah but at what cost?"

$$\text{𝖘} \quad 5 \quad \text{𝖘}$$

.

"**O**hhhh heeeyyy girl!" Zeta yelled as she was about to walk into the Victoria Secret store. She hadn't seen or heard from Jalan in a few days. Normally the two would talk at least once daily. She thought that was odd but chalked it up to the fact that Channing had been with her the last few nights.

After that dreadful night Zeta called Channing and apologized about the embarrassing fiasco. He told her it was okay and that it happened to all women at least once in their lives. Zeta was still baffled at what happened. Her periods were spot on all the time and never wavered. She made an appointment with her gynecologist for the following week.

"Oh hey," Jalan said unenthused. She could feel Shya on the left of her giving her dirty looks. She knew that if the two didn't get away from Zeta and soon Jalan wouldn't be able to control what Shya may end up doing.

"I haven't heard from you in a while, where you been?" Zeta wrapped her arms around Jalan's neck who gave her a half hug with not an ounce of energy behind it.

Zeta didn't take it personal because her conscious wouldn't let her. She knew that what she was doing with Channing was wrong, but she really couldn't help herself. She had never had a man to pay attention to her or show genuine interest in her outside the bedroom and Channing gave her that. The fact that it may ruin the only real friendship that she ever had didn't bother Zeta at all. She wanted what she wanted, and right now that was Channing.

"She's been trying to figure out what her nigga sees in you bitch," Shya said loud enough for Jalan to hear. Jalan threw her a look that said chill and Shya just shrugged her shoulders. She would never understand why her sister was such a pushover when it came to Zeta and Channing. She never stood up for herself with them. Which was the main reason why Shya was always there and ready for whatever.

"I've been trying to find me again, you know. For the last two years or so my life has been revolved around Channing and I let me go. I'm working on fixing that."

"Oh, girl I hear ya, niggas ain't shit anyways." Zeta released a nervous laugh.

"No bitch you ain't shit," Shya countered tucking her hair behind her ear.

"What was that Shya?" Zeta asked with more attitude than Shya was willing to deal with. Zeta knew that Shya didn't care for her and the feelings were mutual. For the sake of Jalan the two merely coexisted when they were put in a position to do so.

Placing her hands on her hips and taking a few steps to close the gaps between her and Zetta, Shya opened her mouth to tell Zeta what she said when the group was interrupted by the presence of two handsome strangers.

For a moment Shya forgot all about her beef with Zeta as the chocolate god from the other night invaded her vision and space. Her eyes traced his dark ones, then down the bridge of his nose, leading to those thick, plump lips that she just wanted to suck on. She discretely squeezed her legs together, but he caught on to the gesture.

"I promise I can handle that for you," Shiloh said before he tucked his bottom lip between his teeth and lightly bit down. It was just something about the funny eyed beauty that drew him to her.

Clearing her throat, Shya crossed her arms across her chest to prevent the sexy specimen in front of her from seeing the fact that she wasn't wearing a bra and she was past turned on. Again, he chuckled at her attempts to keep something from him that he already knew. He had plans on finding her today once he finished up his work. The universe was on his side again because here she was.

"So, I see you did want to see me again." Shya smiled at Shiloh, taking in his athletic physique and the way the thin black t-shirt laid against his chiseled chest that led down to the thick print that was more than visible.

Noticing that Shya's attention had drifted below his waist, Shiloh thrust his hips forward causing a smile to grace her pretty face.

"Damn," slipped past Shiloh's lips.

"Hey, how are you? I'm Zeta." Zeta stepped into Shiloh's view and stuck her hand out in hopes that she would gain his attention. She never missed a chance to be the center of attention and when she wasn't, she did everything in her power to gain it.

Shiloh hated a thirsty female, he felt that it was classless and unladylike. He snarled his nose at her and turned his attention back to Shya, drawing a scoff from Zeta. Her eyes scanned the dark-skinned gentleman and had to admit that he was definitely something to look at. The way his goatee connected with his curly chin hair excited her but the fact he had just dissed her turned her stomach.

"I'm Ziloh," he finally said after damn near staring the clothes off of Jalan. She stood there uncomfortable under his stare, but she didn't want to move either. It was like their energy's matched and it was pulling them together. All she could think about was what their babies would look like.

"I'm Zeta she has a boyfriend," Zeta tried her luck with the other man in attendance. Her phone rung in her hand and she looked to see it was Channing. She debated on whether or not to answer the phone but when Ziloh opened his mouth to speak he made the decision for her.

"Do it look like I'm the kind of man that gives a fuck about another nigga?" The way he lowered his eyes brought an evil feeling into the atmosphere and caused Zeta to pull her hand back and take a step back. She didn't know what was up with these two men but that's something that she had never experienced before.

Men loved Zeta, even if it was just for sexual purposes, they flocked to her. So, the fact that she got dissed by not just one, but both of the male suitors had her self conscious, if only for a second.

"I have to take this," she said as she stepped away from the group to save face. Good thing she did because Shya was two seconds from giving her a piece of her mind. "Hey Boo," she cooed on the phone as Channing answered on the first ring.

"Why didn't you answer the phone when I called Zeta? You know how I feel about that." Zeta rolled her eyes in the back of her head. She didn't understand why Channing was so clingy when it came to her. She never remembered Jalan talking about him being that way, matter of fact is was the exact opposite. Jalan complained about Channing never paying attention to her.

"I was at the mall about to get something sexy for tonight, but I ended up running into Jalan and Shya," Channing groaned on the other end of the phone.

His ego was bruised because he hadn't been home for the last few days, and not once had Jalan picked up the phone to ask him where he was and if he was coming back. In fact, he had called her a few times and never got an answer. He was so conflicted within himself because he wanted to be with other women, but he didn't want Jalan to be with anyone else, even if he didn't want her.

"Oh, okay I'll let you go handle your business, but I'mma see you later right?" Channing asked Zeta. Her eyes darted back to where the sisters were engaged in a full conversation with the rude gentlemen that had joined them before.

"Yeah, my house at eight," she said and then hesitated. Trying to decide if she should tell him about Jalan's newfound attitude, she just couldn't resist the chance to be messy. It just wasn't in her blood to let something like this go. "Um, you won't have a home to go to soon." She chuckled to herself.

Zeta was never taught to be a lady. Her mom taught her to go and get it by any means necessary and to not worry about who she hurt in the process. She knew that if Channing knew that Jalan was out with someone else it would increase her position in his life and she needed that right now even if it was just for the simple fact that she would get to say she took something from Jalan. Plus, after the other night, Zeta was hooked on Channing's dick and she wasn't about to give that up. Friend or not.

"What did you just say?"

"You heard me Channing, Jalan found her a new beau. Not that you care, but yeah, I just met him. He's nice and I guess Shya introduced them because she's with who I assume is his brother. They kinda look a like," she said turning her head to the side to get a better look.

Shya felt someone looking at her and when she turned it was Zeta. That further pissed her off because she felt like Zeta was testing her and she was in the mood to hand out some lessons. Sensing her sister's aggravation, she lightly touched her shoulder and nodded toward the doors of Victoria Secret.

The sisters took off in that direction with the brothers following close behind. Zeta watched as the couples disappeared from her sight but not before Ziloh delivered the most hateful look that caused her to unintentionally shutter under his glare.

"I don't believe you," Channing's words lacked the confidence they once held. He felt like someone punched him in the gut and it wasn't because he was jealous, it was the mere fact that his ego was bruised. Who did Jalan think she was to cheat on him? In his mind none of that worked.

"You don't have to believe me, I can see it with my own eyes," Zeta laughed and headed in the direction to get the proof she felt she needed. "I'll see you at eight, okay?"

Channing didn't say anything, he just hung up the phone and sat back in the chair and ran his hands down his face. He couldn't figure out why he felt the way that he did right now. It was like he was hurt at hearing that Jalan was out with someone else. How could she do that to him? Channing hadn't felt this way about Jalan since they first met, and now he felt like he needed to sit down and talk to her about their relationship.

"I'D LIKE TO SEE YOU IN THIS." SHILOH HELD UP THIS SKIMPY LITTLE black number that left nothing to the imagination. Shya smiled at his insinuation that he would see her in anything other than the clothes on her back.

"Who says you'll be seeing me again after this?" The smile that was permanently plastered on her face was a clear indication that he would be seeing her again and if not, he had ways of making things happen that wouldn't normally happen.

"The fact that since the minute I've been in your space that smile hasn't left your face." He rubbed the back of his hand down the side of her face and she embraced his touch. Normally Shya was strict about her personal space and someone being in hers, but she welcomed Shiloh's invasion more than she would ever want to admit.

"How do you know that smile was for you sir?"

"Because I can feel your energy and I know that our souls are connected, and you know it too." What Shiloh was saying was true, he could feel the connection between the two surge through his body and he couldn't control it. It was like he could feel her heart beating in his chest and that's something that he had never experienced in his 20 years of life.

Shya too felt exactly what Shiloh was talking about. She felt the exact same way which was why she so very much wanted to keep her distance, but something wouldn't let her. She knew that her 21st birthday was on the horizon and she would have to sacrifice a love to give back to the universe, but the more connected she began to feel to this beautiful stranger the more she knew that more than likely she wouldn't be able to do it.

"If you say so," was all she offered Shiloh and he chuckled because he saw everything that she felt in her eyes. He knew that all he needed to do was to get her alone so the two could spend time together and she would be right where he wanted her, in his heart and in his bed.

Shya turned her direction over to her sister who was smiling so big, something that she hadn't seen from Jalan in so long that she almost forgot what it looked like. Watching her sister grab her chest and bend over laughing while Ziloh stared at her like he was trying to figure out what was so funny caused a light giggle to leave Shya's lips.

"You know if you let me, I can break all those walls you got built up around your heart for you." Shya didn't even know that Shiloh had walked up behind her until she felt the warmth of his breath on the nape of her neck.

Slithering his arms around her waist and pulling her back to him, Shya tried to resist but in reality, she didn't want to. She wanted to know what it felt like to indulge in a night of fun and to see if Shiloh was everything that she thought he was. She knew that in her *culture* this was frowned upon but right now she didn't care.

Glancing to the left, she saw Zeta with her phone up snapping pictures and that lit something in her that she had to release. "I'll be right back." She tapped on Shiloh's arm and he reluctantly let her go. Jalan felt a surge of energy as she normally does when Shya is about to explode and she turned in the direction of where her sister was just standing.

"Where'd she go?" Jalan asked frantically. Shiloh looked around and didn't see her anywhere. He knew that he had just turned his head for a second and then she was gone. Jalan put her head in her hands and made a quick wish that her sister didn't do anything that would put them in a bad position.

On the other side of the store, Shya hid behind a rack of clothes. She had just thought of the perfect spell, but she didn't want to chance anyone hearing her say it, so she went to hide. She could see her sister looking for her and Shiloh had scanned the area once or twice himself. There was only a matter of time before Jalan found her sibling and Shya knew it.

> *"You're nothing but a dirty whore,*
> *who loves to take what is not yours.*
> *Trifling, dumb and fake as hell,*
> *I hope that nigga's got your bail."*

Tucking her hair behind her right ear, she was satisfied with the task at hand. She took the long way around to where the group was about to send out a search party for her. Shya rejoined the group and slipped right back into Shiloh's arms where she was before she left to go handle business.

"Where were you?" Jalan asked her sister knowing her too well.

"Hey y'all, sorry that was my new boo calling, I needed to holla at him. He's planning a really special evening for the two of us. Jalan you gone help me pick out something sexy?" Zeta asked pulling Jalan away from the handsome stranger who had no plans on letting Jalan get out of his sight.

It had been a while since Ziloh had someone that he was interested in for more than sex. He wanted to get to know Jalan. He felt that she had more to offer than just sex, but he could also feel there was a barrier up and he could bet that it had to do with the boyfriend that the aggravating friend was talking about.

"I don't think that anything in here will make you sexy to be real," Ziloh said with a shrug of his shoulders. "Your spirit is ugly ma so that makes you ugly." Ziloh was never one to bite his tongue. The sight of Zeta was putting him in a bad mood and he didn't want that. He wanted to chill and have some fun with his brother and the beautiful sisters.

Zeta looked at herself in the mirror trying to figure out what Ziloh was talking about. She was far from ugly and any man would tell you that. *He must be gay,* she thought to herself. The distressed jeans that she had on made her medium sized ass look more plump, and her washboard stomach accentuated her c-cup breast. Her short pixie cut that she had just got made her face slender and brought out the length of her eyelashes that she paid for. Her cinnamon colored skin was blemish free and smooth. She couldn't find one flaw in her appearance, not one at all.

"Yo you a ditzy bitch too," Shiloh said causing Shya to laugh out loud, drawing in an evil stare from Zeta. "He saying you're all surface, there's no depth to you. Do you understand?" Shiloh waited for an answer that he knew he would never get. Zeta just glared at him with a blank stare because to be honest she didn't give a fuck what they were saying because in her mind if they didn't want her, they were gay. "Bet!" was all he said. "You ready to roll out?" He looked down at Shya.

Shiloh had plans of taking Shya back to the house he shared with his brother and spending some time with her. He just wanted to know more about the woman who had stolen his heart and held it captive for the last couple of days. He needed to know if what he felt was as real as it felt and the only way he would know that was by spending time with her.

"You trying to kidnap me ain't you?" Shya said, actually excited about the fact that she was about to spend time with Shiloh. A part of her wanted to play hard to get but she couldn't, not with him. The words would never leave her lips. It's like whatever he said went and she wasn't even trying to fight it.

"Yep," was all that Shiloh offered.

"You rolling right?" Ziloh asked Jalan and she nodded. Not in the mood to go to her empty house and stress about where Channing was and who he was with. She was sure that tonight would be spent with Zeta seeing as though she was here to buy a sexy outfit. Shaking the thoughts from her head she smiled in Zeta's direction.

"So, you just going home with a man that you don't even know when you gotta a man at home?" Zeta asked.

"You really worried about my man at home. If you really need to know my man ain't been home in a few days, you wouldn't happen to know anything about that, now would you?"

Jalan hated confrontation for the simple fact she knew how mad she could get and when she got there, it wasn't much that could calm her down or stop her from using magic in public and she didn't want that again. Zeta, however was testing every nerve she had in her body. She was just about tired of this charade with her anyway.

"What? Why would I know anything about Channing?" she asked as if she was offended that Jalan would ask such a thing. Shya scoffed and rolled her eyes at Zeta's Oscar winning performance that she was putting on. "I would never do that to you Jalan, I may be a lot of things, but a bad friend is not one of them."

Everyone that was standing there burst out laughing, before they headed for the door to walk out of the store. Zeta followed in behind them pleading her case and when she walked through the door to exit the detectors started going off.

The group stopped in their tracks, Jalan shot Shya a look trying to see if she had anything to do with this but Shya's face was void of any emotions.

"Ma'am," the store manager called out. "I need to look in your bag."

"Look in my bag for what?" Zeta yelled out. "I don't steal." If looks could kill Zeta would have the family of the store manager, whose name tag read Lisa, planning a funeral soon.

Not wanting to further cause a scene, Zeta handed over her bag that all of a sudden felt heavier than before. She looked on as the store manager opened the bag and then looked up at her with a smirk on her face.

"You don't steal huh?" there was humor in her voice because the employee will get a small bonus for catching someone stealing merchandise and she was excited about it because Halloween was near-ing, and she had yet to get her kids costumes.

One by one she began to pull out bras, panties, a few nighties and some lingerie. There was so much stuff in there everyone looked on with wide eyes except for Shya. She wanted to make sure that Zeta was in jail at least for the night.

The group watched as the manager called for store security as Zeta begged and pleaded, trying to convince them that it wasn't her and that she was innocent. The cries and pleas fell on deaf ears, but it didn't stop her from trying it.

"Damn shorty got sticky fingers?" Shiloh said watching the scene unfold not knowing that Shya was the culprit behind the madness but Jalan knew which was why she was staring a hole in her sister who refused to look in her direction.

"Yeah looks like it." Shya smiled and leaned her body into Shiloh who accepted her with open arms. From the outside looking in, no one would ever guess the couple had just met days ago.

❦ 6 ❧

After watching the police arrest Zeta, everyone decided that they wanted to shop for what they initially came to the mall for. The four dipped in and out of the different stores racking up bag after bag, just enjoying the company of one another.

Shiloh had learned that Shya was too about to turn 21 and the two shared the same birthday, both born on Halloween. They had so much in common that neither of them could believe that the other was real.

"Damn what are the odd's that I see you here? I think it's fate, what do you think?" Tanala, the girl from Club Met that couldn't catch a hint walked up to Shiloh and Ziloh while the girls dipped into the bathroom for a second.

Shya was oblivious to the drama that she was about to walk into, she was on an emotional high right now. Everything about today brought her nothing but joy and she was determined to keep it that way, until her sister opened her mouth.

"He might be the one Shya," Jalan said not purposely trying to ruin the mood but she was successful nonetheless. "He's really feeling you."

"Really bitch?" Shya's hands went on her hips and her lips were a mile long she was so mad at her sister's attempt to ruin her night.

"I'm sorry Shya, I just wanted to throw that out there."

"Why, because you know that you're stuck in a bullshit ass relationship with Channing who's fucking your best friend? So, you're miserable and you want me to be miserable too?" Shya shouted. Not intending to hit below the belt, but she was pissed the fuck off. Her day was damn near perfect until this moment. "For once I just want to feel fucking normal. I don't want to be reminded of that shit every time you turn around."

"I'm sorry Shya but it's your fucking reality. I don't want to lose you and that's what's gonna happen if you don't get your head out of you ass and do what you have to do. Cut him off and find someone else if you don't want that but you know it has to be genuine and that nigga got ya nose wide open so no one else will be able to come in and compare."

Jalan's words were honest, she wasn't trying to piss her sister off, but her sister was more important than any stranger that they just met. She needed her to understand that the love ritual wasn't something that she could play with. The universe blessed us with powers and we had to repay it and sacrificing love was the highest form of payment.

"Whatever, I'm just ready to go home. I don't want to be around anybody right now." Shya rolled her eyes and pushed her way out of the bathroom right into a bunch of mess.

"Look I told you one time you ain't got shit for me. I don't know what part of that shit you don't understand. Like you trying to piss me the fuck off right now."

"Oh, so this why you tripping?" Tanala just couldn't believe that he wanted nothing to do with her. She just couldn't wrap her mind around that, she never had an issue around the hood getting men so why he was dissing her was foreign to her. In her mind, it had to do with the freaky eyed bitch. She was the only reason he wouldn't give her any play.

"You ever thought about the fact he just don't find you attractive? I mean he seems to like a little ass and nice size breasts, a pretty face. You know shit like that, shit that you don't possess," Shya said as her hands explored her body and had Shiloh in a trance, every body part she described her hands went there and so did Shiloh's eyes.

His dick grew to full potential and he had no plans to hide it as it commanded the attention of both Shya and Tanala. No one ever noticed the friends that were lagging behind Tanala finally catch up with lust dancing around their eyes. They knew money when they saw it and the men in front of them bathed in it.

"Oh no, I'm damn sure gone get me some of that." Tanala reached out to grab his dick but he caught her wrists. He didn't understand what was wrong with this girl who he's told on more than one occasion that he didn't want her, and she was still coming on strong.

He knew just the thing to get her to chill out, literally. "You look a little hot," he said right before he grabbed his dick and did an adjustment.

A weird feeling came over Tanala as she jerked her hand away from Shiloh. She all of the sudden felt hot and she couldn't fight the urge to take off her clothes. No matter how much she was telling her hands to stop they wouldn't, it was like they had a mind of their own.

The worry lines on her forehead brought on a smile from Shiloh as he watched her try and fight against the spell and ultimately lose. Piece by piece she began to undress herself until she was ass naked in the middle of the mall.

Shya looked on in confusion as to why a woman would degrade herself in front of all of these people just to get a man's attention. "You are one dumb bitch, because the nigga don't want you, you just gonna strip ass naked." She furrowed her eyebrows. "The least you could have done was shave your cat if you were gone be putting on shows." Shya's frown deepened as her eyes traveled down to Tanala's private area that looked like it's never seen a razor

"Fuck you bitch, why you worried about me? Your nigga seems to like it."

Before Shya could say anything, mall security ran over to where they were and attempted to make her get dressed. A small crowd had circled around and the majority of them had their phones out.

> *"Throw that ass in a circle,*
> *throw it like you on a mission.*
> *Bend it over bust it open,*
> *since you like the attention,"*

Shya said low enough that no one heard her, everyone was too busy watching the show to see what she was doing. She tucked her hair behind her right ear and watched as Tanala started to twerk uncontrollably. Placing her hands on her knees she popped what little ass she did have. The mall cop tried his best to get her under control but to no avail. The crowd had doubled in size and they were all taking videos and pictures.

"Shya stop it!" Jalan whispered in her ear. She tried to sound stern, but she could hear the humor in her tone. Unable to hold it in Jalan burst out laughing and the two sisters enjoyed a minute of fun.

Tanala's friends just stood there unsure of what to do. They had never seen their friend act like that. True she slept around and would do almost anything for a man's attention but the three of them were in agreement that this was way too far. Finally, they stepped up and tried to help her get dressed but she couldn't stop moving.

Enough of the bullshit, Shiloh grabbed his dick again and she stopped in her tracks and looked around at everyone looking at her and then she looked down at herself realizing she was naked. Tanala screamed and grabbed her clothes and dipped into the bathroom. She had never felt that disconnected with her body before and she had taken some pretty strong drugs.

"What the fuck was that?" Ziloh said unable to control his laughter. He was bent over while Jalan rubbed his back and shook her head still trying to keep her composure. Shiloh and Shya both smiled knowing that they were the ones to cause the chaos and no one knew about it, not even each other.

"She said she was putting on shows for that dick," Shya said with a smirk on her face. "Let me find out the D got 'em going crazy."

Leaning down so that only she could hear him, "Play ya cards right and you'll find out tonight." Tucking her bottom lip in between her teeth she silently hoped that would be the case. It had been a while since Shya had a good fuck. She needed something to take her mind away from the situation that was quickly approaching.

"Shit that was funny." Ziloh finally came up for air as the group got closer to the door. That was the funniest thing that he had saw in a long time and he knew his brother had something to do with it, at least her getting naked. He saw that part but what was baffling to him was the dancing, his brother didn't do that so either that bitch was really trying to get attention or someone else had something to do with that.

"You okay?" Jalan asked Ziloh, the way her voice flowed through his ears brought on a serious expression on his face. Jalan was hurt and there were hints of that in every word that she spoke.

"Are you okay?" Ziloh asked and Jalan knew exactly what he meant. He knew he heard the back and forth between her and Zeta. Even though he didn't mention it, it had been on his mind since the argument. It was weird to him that she was so calm about the whole situation. Most women would be freaking out or trying to fight but not her, and that piqued his interest.

"Yeah, I'm good. Sometimes you need to see certain things to get you out of certain head spaces you know? Annnnnnnnnnd not every action deserves a reaction from me." She tilted her head to the side and Ziloh nodded his head. When she was ready to open up to him about the situation she would, so for right now he would let it be.

$\mathcal{H}$ 7 $\mathcal{H}$

"**D**amn this is nice," Shya said as they crossed the threshold of the brothers' mansion. The house that they shared was two houses combined by a central living room that had a long hallway extending from each side. The houses had 4-bedrooms and 4-bathrooms, each built to the brothers' liking.

"Thank you," Ziloh said smiling and slipping his hands into his pockets. His eyes diverted to Jalan who seemed to be deep in thought as she surveyed her surroundings. "You're safe here, well for the most part." A slight chuckle left his lips.

"Do I even want to know what that means?" she shook her head. Her mind was on the fact that she was here with another man willingly. Shya didn't even have to talk her into it, matter of fact she was the one that suggested that the night not end. No one objected but she brought the idea to the forefront. The crazy part about it all was that she wasn't regretting it not one bit.

Like Shya said, she just wanted to live normal, if only for one night. So tonight, she was letting her hair down and enjoying the chocolate god standing in front of her.

"Oh, you'll find out when we step into my domain," Ziloh said under his breath but Jalan heard him and flashed a smile. What he didn't know was that Jalan had the sexual appetite of an 18-year-old boy that she's been keeping bottled up for the last two years because her boyfriend would rather find solace in other women than to have sex with his girlfriend.

Jalan can't remember the last time she had meaningful sex, sex that she was able to release all the stress that she had pent up. She was definitely looking forward to a night to remember.

"You okay sister?" Shya asked surprised that Jalan hadn't bolted yet. She was just waiting for her sister to say they had to go so she could go home and wait on Channing who wouldn't be there because he had to go pick his bitch up from jail.

"Yeah why?" Jalan asked with a confused look on her face.

"I was just asking." Shya threw her hands up in mock surrender and Jalan shook her head with a smirk.

"I just want to let my hair down and..."

"Get some dick!" Shiloh interrupted. He was finishing Jalan's sentence, but his eyes were dead set on Shya's and his statement was to her.

He was so physically and emotionally attracted to her that it almost hurt that he couldn't be inside her, and he needed to relieve that pain. He needed to satisfy the hunger that he had for her. The way she was looking at him said she needed the same thing.

"You sure you good sis?" Shya asked wanting to make sure that her sister would be okay because she didn't want to seem selfish, but she had a desire burning inside and there was only one thing that could put it out and it was attached to the man standing in front of her.

Shya couldn't explain the attraction that she felt, and the fact that it was more than sexual made it that much better. The time they spent getting to know each other at the mall was something out of a movie. She just kept telling herself that nothing is ever that perfect, that there had to be something wrong with him.

Truth was, there was nothing wrong with Shiloh except for the fact that he held the same secret as she did.

"Yeah take yo hot ass on Shya." She laughed and Shya gave her a thumbs up and her and Shiloh disappeared down the long hallway.

An uncomfortable silence filled the room, Jalan wasn't used to being in the presence of a man outside of Channing. Although she wanted to be here, she couldn't help the tinge of guilt that kept pulling at her heart. Even though he didn't give a damn about her, she prided herself on being loyal.

"I think you being loyal to the wrong person," Ziloh said reading her mind. He knew that she was feeling guilty about being there, but she shouldn't be. He was hoping that she would loosen up soon because he was really enjoying being around her and he didn't want that to end. "Tell me about it."

"Tell you about what?" Jalan turned to face Ziloh who had his hands tucked away deep in his pockets. He was trying his hardest to keep his hands to himself, knowing that right now what she needs is someone to listen to her and be there, but the shit was hard.

From her curly crazy hair to the slight bow of her legs, everything about this woman was perfect. Even damaged she was perfect.

"I want to know why he's sleeping with your best friend." Ziloh got right to the point. He didn't feel like there was a reason for him to beat around the bush. He wanted to know what made her tick and what things he should avoid so he can try and make her happy.

"Let's just say, I tried to *make* him love me and I shouldn't have. I should have let love come naturally but I just had to do it my way and it backfired and hard. Now I have to accept the things that I set into motion."

"You don't have to accept that shit, that's bullshit!" for some reason hearing her say that enraged him slightly and he wanted to reach out and shake her for a second, but he refrained in fear that he may scare her off. "Just because you made a mistake doesn't mean that you have to deal with it, just leave. Fuck him! Let that hoe have him."

"Calm down handsome," she giggled. "I just felt like I needed to live in my karma you know?" She didn't quite know how to explain the situation without coming out and saying *hey I cast a spell that back fired because my ass knew not to use my powers for romantic gain.* So, she had to keep it as simple as possible.

"No, I don't know!" Jerica had been the only woman that ever came close to owning his heart and when she died so did any desire for him to love again. Having to sacrifice her damn near killed every monogamous thought in his heart but here he was looking into the eyes of Jalan trying to figure out how he can rearrange his life to fit her in. "Do you love him?"

"I thought I did, but the more I think about it I feel like our whole situation was more about proving my mother wrong and fixing my mistakes. Like I said, I was trying to live in my karma."

The honesty in her tone made Ziloh want to reach out and take all the pain that's she's ever felt away. He knew if given the chance they could possibly make each other happy but first they needed to figure out a way to get her mind off of the shit with, who Ziloh is referring to as her ex, did.

"Come here," Ziloh motioned for her to come closer to him. Hesitating, Jalan took slow and deliberate steps in the direction of the sexy man that was sure to take her out of her element.

The moment that she was in his space he enclosed her in his arms and pulled her to him. She took a whiff of his cologne and drifted off into a place of peace and love, a place that she had never been. For the first time in her adult life she felt safe and happy, she knew right then that she didn't want to lose that.

Looking up in the eyes of the man that was causing foreign feelings to invade her heart, she noticed something in him that she couldn't quite put her finger on. All she knew was that it was intriguing and if she could help it, she would be getting a crash course in all things Ziloh.

"I want you to make love to me," Jalan allowed to slip out of her lips. Her eyes stretched wide because she was shocked that she allowed that to come out of her mouth. She was never the one to be so forward and forthcoming about her wants and needs, especially in the bedroom.

Ziloh let the words that she had just spoken marinate. He so badly wanted to snatch her up and throw her over the couch, grab a handful of hair and fuck the shit out of her while she screams out his name until she's hoarse. But Ziloh knew that she was dealing with the bullshit her ex did to her and him taking her body would only complicate that, so he practiced a little self control and pressed his lips on her forehead.

The feeling of embarrassment flushed over her and she cleared her throat to clear some space in the now thick room. She felt stupid for throwing herself out there to only be rejected. Attempting to pull away from Ziloh, he tightened his grip and turned her so that her back was to his chest. He rested his chin on the top of her head while he sighed heavily trying to think of anything besides the fact that she was so close to him.

He needed to think of the right thing to say so that she understood where he was coming from and so that he convinced himself not to take it there knowing that it could possibly interfere with what he was hoping would come out of this.

"I'm sorry, I—I didn't mean to come off like that I—I just—" Jalan tried to explain but Ziloh cut her off by leaning down and crashing his lips against hers.

What was meant to be a way to show her that he was indeed interested but for her sake, he was trying to refrain from knocking her down and possibly fucking her head up even worse than ol boy had done, turned into a passion filled kissed that neither of them wanted to break away from.

"Wait hold up." Ziloh grabbed her shoulders and pulled her back from his lips. "Fuck!" his eyes went to the ceiling as he willed his dick to stop throbbing with anticipation of something that he wasn't gonna get. "Got damn."

"I need this, even if it's just one night and I never see you again I want to feel you." Her sultry voice flowed through his ear, down his body and right to the tip of his dick.

"No!" he yelled more to convince himself. The saddened look that took over her face made him feel like shit. He didn't want her to think that he wasn't attracted to her or that he didn't want to be with her. That was the furthest thing from the truth, but he knew that him fucking her right now would damage her more than that fuck nigga already had. "I know that if this goes down there is no way that I will be able to just settle for one night. I haven't even been inside you and I can already tell that you about to fuck a nigga head up. And before I allow you to do that, I need to make sure that ol' boy is out of your system. I won't share, I'm selfish as fuck and things can get real ugly if someone interferes with that."

Jalan's eyes bounced around his as she tried to find the right words to say. She so badly wanted to tell him that she was done with Channing and that there was nothing left for them. That would have been partly true, but she still hadn't been granted the closure that she needed.

"You're right," she said in a defeated tone. "Let me go get my sister and see if she's ready to go."

"Oh, so just because I ain't busting down ya walls you gotta leave?" Ziloh gave her a hateful look that caused a soft giggle to escape her lips. "So, you was just gone hit and quit? You that cold Jalan?"

"No," the giggle that she was trying to suppress turned into a full fledge laugh as he deepened the scowl on his face. "I just didn't think you wanted anything else." Shyly tucking her hair behind her ear, she waited for Ziloh to respond.

"Normally that would be the case, but you're different." Grabbing her hand Ziloh escorted Jalan down the long hallway to his house and back to his bedroom. Jalan's heart began to beat out of control, she swallowed hard trying to calm her nerves.

Ziloh was steady trying to figure out where this new-found strength came from because his dick is the one thing he has never been able to control. Being around Jalan today opened his mind up to something other than the way that a woman felt. It was something about her energy that drew him to her and he planned on making sure that the feeling that he was feeling was one that would be around for a while.

"What did you mean by *normally?*" Jalan asked not really interested in the answer but needed something to get her mind off the fact that she was standing in the middle of this man's home, a man that she knew nothing about other than the fact that he was fine as hell and she was drawn to him.

"It means that normally I'm not up for the conversation or the woman's feelings. I'm okay with them bent over and their face in a pillow so I won't have to hear their voices," he said honestly. Jalan cleared her throat, unsure if she was okay with what he was saying, she was going through the same thing with Channing right now. She asked herself over and over if she could handle being with someone like that again. "Don't over think it beautiful, they didn't respect themselves, so none came from me."

"Oh okay," was all she offered.

Instead of trying to explain, Ziloh stripped down to his boxers and handed Jalan a t-shirt from his drawer. He pointed to the bathroom where she could go and change and get comfortable. She didn't know if she could be this close to him with out wanting more than he was willing to give but it looks like she didn't have a choice.

After she was dressed down and more comfortable, she walked out of the bathroom and climbed in the bed where a waiting Ziloh was awaiting her return. She laid on her back a good way away from Ziloh and he chuckled, pulling her closer.

"I promise you a sample of the dick as soon as you ain't fucking with that nigga no more."

"Well I don't want it if you spreading it around," she said sarcastically.

"Let's just see if you have the power to make that happen," he whispered in her ear and turned her so that her back was to his chest. Pulling her as close as he could, he nestled his head in her neck and drifted off to sleep.

His last words played over and over in Jalan's head. She did have the power to make that happen but that's what got her in the situation that she was in now. Exhaling softly, she drifted off into the most peaceful sleep that she's had in years.

✾ 8 ✾

"So, tell me something about Shiloh that I don't already know," Shya said sitting with her back against the headboard of his cherry oak sleigh bed. She had been trying to control her emotions from the minute she walked in the room, but it was becoming harder and harder. The longer that she was in his presence the more she wanted him. She was hoping that indulging in a conversation would keep her yearning at bay.

"You're stalling," Shiloh's voice was low and throaty further adding to the lust that filled the room. He knew exactly what Shya wanted but he thought that it would be more fun for her to ask for it or take it, either way would give him the pleasure he was seeking.

"Stalling?" She released a nervous laugh causing a chuckle to escape Shiloh's lips. His eyes were low and inviting. Shya has never been the one to shy away from a man but she felt herself blushing and her stomach filling with butterflies.

Her mom always told her that her body would let her know when she found the one, she would not be able to control herself and she'd crave the affection and attention of him. Exactly what she was experiencing right now.

"Yes stalling, all you have to do is say the word and I'll do everything that has been going through your mind since we walked in this room." Dragging his tongue along his bottom lip he pulled it in his mouth.

Shya had to squeeze her legs together to keep from soaking his bed. She was only donned in a long t-shirt and a pair of thongs. She hated to wear bras and the shirt that she chose to wear today didn't require one, so she opted against wearing one. She felt exposed under his stare and he knew it which is why he zoned in on her nipples that were about to pop out of the shirt that she was wearing.

"Humph."

"Humph?" Shiloh teased. "You're sexy in my shirt. You should wear them more often."

"Play your cards right and I will."

"Play my cards right?" Shiloh's right eyebrow shot up and a smirk appeared on his face. He planned on playing every card he was dealt when it came to the beautiful woman occupying his space. Their connection was both physical and emotional, something that neither of the two had ever experienced.

When something felt right to Shya she normally went with it, and this felt right to her so whatever happened tonight she believed was meant to be and she was damn sure opened to it. Shya nodded her head at Shiloh's question and that gave him the green light to do what he had been anticipating all night.

Grabbing her by the legs, he jerked her down so that she was lying flat on her back. He ran his hands from her thighs to her hips and then back down. Enjoying the feel of her smooth buttery skin, he traveled up further until his hands were under the shirt.

"Mmmm," fell through her lips as she arched her back the minute his hands were on her breast and her nipple was between his thumb and index finger.

Just hearing the sound of her moans took Shiloh over the edge and he couldn't take it anymore, he needed to feel her. Sliding the shirt that she was wearing over her head he had to stop and take in the masterpiece that was before him.

"You're fucking beautiful."

Shya could hear the passion in his words, she leaned up so that her mouth could connect with his. The energy in the room was so high that the two couldn't help but get lost in it. Their tongues danced around while they tried their best to show what they were feeling in the moment.

Placing his finger in the band of her thongs he worked them down, lifting just enough to get them off along with the basketball shorts that he had on. Never breaking the kiss, he wedged himself between her legs.

"You sure about this?" he asked, silently praying that she didn't change her mind. When she reached down and placed his monster at her opening, he helped her by sliding in her tight, warm, wet walls.

The feeling that moved through him was something out of this world. It was like he was having an outer body experience as he worked his way in and out of her at a slow steady pace, until he was fully inside of her.

Shya wore the look of pain on her face as she waited for it to subside and the pleasure to kick in. She wasn't a virgin by far, but Shiloh was the biggest that had ever crossed her threshold, but she was determined to take it and have fun with it as soon as it stopped feeling like it was gonna rip her insides out.

"Sssssssss." Biting her bottom lip, Shya pressed her head into the pillow that she was laying on as the first wave of ecstasy flowed through her body, exactly what she's been wanting. "Shit that feels good, Shiloh."

"You say my name like that again, I'll have to show you what you been missing in your life," he taunted but what he didn't know was that Shya was always down for a challenge and she damn sure loved a good time.

"Show me nigga." A slow and controlled smile spread across her face and Shiloh had to bite his bottom lip to keep from releasing every seed he housed in his nuts inside of her at that moment.

"That mouth gone get you in a world of trouble," he leaned down and whispered in her ear and the warmth of his breath tickled her ear and she moaned unintentionally.

"I can back it up."

"Bet!"

Leaning back, Shiloh put Shya's legs in the crook of his arms and pushed them back towards her head. In the push up position, he wound his hips into her, making sure to grind as far as he could into her.

"Fuck!" Shya yelled out as she felt a surge of pleasure shoot through her body. Throwing her body in his direction, matching him stroke for stroke, Shya could feel the sweat forming on her brow. Her breathing picked up and she was about to cum and no matter how hard she was trying to hold it she just couldn't.

"Don't hold shit back from me," Shiloh growled as he continued to work the shit out of Shya's pussy. "Damn yo shit good!"

"Best you ever had?"

"Best I ever fucking had. Got damn!"

Getting on his knees and taking his hands he pressed Shya's thighs back and out, so he had the perfect view of her perfect pussy. He had to bite his lip again, shaking his head and speeding up his thrusts. The minute he began to thumb her clit, Shya lost it. She yelled out so many obscenities so fast that neither of them knew exactly what she said.

"Shit you're gonna make me cum so damn hard." She shut her eyes as she felt herself about to explode.

"Open your eyes Shya, I wanna see how I make you feel." Shaking her head, no she squeezed them tighter. Not one to be told no Shiloh pulled all the way out of her and slammed back in causing Shya's eyes to pop open. "You didn't hear me?"

"Oh my god, this feels so got damn good! Shit right there!"

"Where, right here?" he angled himself and attacked the gushy spot that his dick had suddenly become attached to. "Shit Shya!"

Sucking his bottom lip in between his teeth he released her clit and concentrated on his strokes. He was close and wanted to make sure that they experienced the magic together.

"I'm about to, oh shit!"

"Fuck man!" Shiloh yelled out at the same time.

The lights began to flicker and things on the dresser shifted back and forth involuntarily. The headboard started to shake vigorously as the couple continued to please each other to the best of their ability, completely oblivious to the chaos around them.

"I'm coming baby, fuck I'm coming!" Shya's nails embedded themselves into Shiloh's shoulder and her eyes found their place in the back of her head as her toes curled, legs began to shake, and her stomach tightened. "Yes, shit yes!"

"Fuck, I'm nutting!" Shiloh yelled out as they both released, causing the bulb in the lamp to shatter and the bed to come crashing to the floor. They both looked around completely out of breath and unsure of what happened.

When their eyes met each other's they both burst out laughing. Neither of them had ever had that happen. Shya was somewhat embarrassed at the fact that she came so hard that she caused the bed to break, meanwhile Shiloh was thinking the same thing. The weird part about the whole thing was neither of them seemed thrown off about it and that made what had just happened that much better.

"Damn that was one hell of an orgasm," Shya said trying to break the ice of the events following.

"Fuck yeah, a nigga ain't never broke a bed before." The two laughed again before Shiloh got serious again. "I don't know what it is about you, but I need your energy in my life, your vibe is like nothing in this world."

Shya swallowed hard because although she felt the same, she knew that if she continued on with this that she would have to sacrifice the love that she could possibly have in him. She smiled and bit her lip.

"Me too," was all she offered before their lips connected again. Shya knew that there was no way that she would ever be able to give him to the universe so to avoid that, tonight would be the last time she saw him.

❦ 9 ❧

Channing sat on the edge of the bed wondering where Jalan was and why she didn't come home last night. When he went to pick Zeta up from jail, she showed him the pictures of Jalan and the man he knew as Ziloh, his connect.

Channing had been copping his drugs from Ziloh and Shiloh for years. They had the best coke and weed on the east coast, at the best prices. They were the reason that Channing was so successful in what he did and was able to make the money he did. He was able to charge out the ass for the product because it was such good quality, but he barely paid anything for it, so he double his profit.

"How in the fuck does she even know him?" he asked himself throwing his head in his hands. This shit was putting him in a bad position, if he went to Ziloh on some rah rah shit he would be losing out on money, but he couldn't just let the fact that he was sleeping with his woman go that easily.

He needed to talk to Jalan and see where her head was. He didn't understand why all of a sudden her feelings mattered to him, but they did and the thought of losing her was now an issue for him.

Hearing the door open and shut, he jumped up to go and meet with Jalan, who could care less if Channing was home or not. She saw his car outside, but she was in the best of moods and didn't want to let anyone ruin that for her.

Ziloh was the perfect gentlemen and even though she wanted him to fuck her until she passed out, she understood why he didn't and that made her respect him even more. She was so excited to see him again tonight that she was already mentally preparing for her date that was almost 12 hours away.

"Where have you been Jalan? It's nine o'clock in the damn morning and you're just now strolling in the house?"

If Jalan didn't know any better than she would have sworn that Channing actually gave a damn about her, but she knew that it couldn't be. The day she cast the spell for him to love her was the day that anything they could have possibly had was over. She never understood why she did what she did. In her mind she could change his mind with love and ended up hurting herself.

"I was out Channing, how was your night?"

Swallowing hard, he tried to figure out why he all of a sudden he cared what Jalan thought about what he did when he wasn't with her. She wasn't the woman that he wanted, Zeta was so why in the hell did he have a feeling in the pit of his stomach telling him to make up a good lie, so she didn't leave him.

"I was here waiting on you, trying to figure out a way to make us work. That's how my night went."

"You don't even lie good anymore." Jalan shook her head and headed to the bathroom. When she walked past Channing, he faintly smelled the scent of cologne, a scent that he wasn't familiar with and definitely didn't belong to him.

"You smell like a man." He grabbed her arm and jerked her to him. The scowl that formed on his face put caution in Jalan's heart. Channing had never put his hands on her or even raised his voice for that matter, so his actions were completely out of character. She didn't understand what the hell was going on with him.

"I suggest you let me go before you make me do something that we both may regret."

Slowly releasing her arm, Channing gave her a pleading look and she almost felt bad for him until she remembered seeing him out with her best friend like they were a couple. Speaking of Zeta, she had been calling and texting Jalan nonstop, her last message said that she had something important to tell her but right now wasn't the time.

"Listen Jalan, I want us to sit down and talk about this. I miss you and I miss us, I think we can fix this. I want us to go back to what we use to be." He smiled and ran his hand down the side of her face.

Closing her eyes, she relished in his touch, it was everything that she's wanted for so long. Was it possible that he could finally be becoming the man that she thought he could be? Or was this some kind of wicked trick from the universe?

"Channing..." Jalan started and then shook her head. She backed away from where he was standing. The only thing that kept running through her mind was seeing him with Zeta. There was no way that she would be able to get past that. That was her best friend, her sister. How could she ever look at the two again?

"Is he the reason?" he said pulling his phone out of his back pocket. "He is the reason you don't want to fix us?" he turned the picture around to where Jalan could see its contents. She gasped and covered her hand with her mouth.

"Where did you get those pictures?" she asked already knowing the answer, she just wanted to hear it from him.

"It doesn't matter where I got them, why were you with him? Do you even know who he is?" the hurt expression made Jalan feel bad, that wasn't who she was, and she totally acted out of character last night and the worst part was she didn't regret it at all. She wanted Ziloh and she didn't think anyone or anything would be able to change that.

"I don't have time for this, I'm tired and I'm not about to let you ruin my good mood." She pushed past him, before she got to the room she turned and looked back at him. "Did Zeta get out last night, cause I'm sure that's how you got the pictures." Channing opened his mouth and closed it again. He shook his head to try and indicate that Jalan was wrong because the words wouldn't leave his mouth. Jalan laughed and nodded her head. "Yeah okay."

The tight white jeans that Jalan wore made her ass sit up nicely and as she walked away Channing's eyes were glued to it. He knew that he needed to take things into his own hands. If she didn't want to talk about her being with Ziloh then he would just go and talk to Ziloh. He didn't want to fuck up how he made his money, but he wasn't about to let him take his girl either. He couldn't have that.

"Hey Jalan, I'll be back," he yelled into the room. He wasn't expecting an answer and he didn't receive one.

Zeta was now an issue for him and he needed to cut ties with her at least until he could get Jalan back in his good graces.

"YOU TRYING TO TELL ME YOU DIDN'T HIT?" SHILOH STOOD IN front of his brother with his arms folded and his lips twisted not believing anything that he was saying.

Shiloh knew his brother and he knew that if he had the chance to fuck a girl, he was fucking no questions asked. Sex was like air to that nigga and he had to have that shit. So, the fact that he was saying that Jalan asked him to beat it up and he turned her down to cuddle was baffling to him.

"Seriously, she didn't need that. I knew that if I would have fucked the shit out of her, she would have looked at me like that bitch ass nigga she with and it wouldn't have gone anywhere. Right now, he's fucking her over. Just fuck her and doing his thing. He don't give a fuck about her. She's a good ass girl and we click. I wanted her to feel something different." He shrugged his shoulders like what he was saying was normal.

"You in love or some shit? I ain't never heard you say no shit like that." Shiloh was confused at his brothers new found feelings, he didn't think the nigga had them.

"Fuck you nigga." He flipped him off, but the confusion plastered on Shiloh's face never wavered. He shook his head and sighed. "I'm feeling the fuck out of her vibe and I can't explain the shit. I just feel like the universe sent her my way. Shit weird as fuck but it's like I can't turn that bullshit off, not that I want to."

"I feel that," Shiloh said.

He too was feeling the same way, but he was just scared that the universe sent her so that he could sacrifice her, and he didn't think he could do that. His birthday was in two weeks and he still hadn't found a recipient for the Love Ritual. As bad as he wanted to go out and find someone his conscious wouldn't let him do it. The only girl on his mind was Shya and he wasn't about to change that, not even for the universe. As if reading his mind.

"Ya birthday is less than two weeks away Shiloh."

"Don't fucking start that bullshit." Shiloh walked away from where he was just standing talking to his brother. He was already battling with the inevitable within himself, he didn't need his brother reminding him of the shit.

"Nigga don't get mad at me. I already had to do the shit. Hell, you ain't no better than me. The shit is fucked up but ain't no way around the shit!" Ziloh yelled and Shiloh waved him off. He didn't even bother to respond.

He was trying to think of a way to avoid having to give up the one thing that felt different for him. Going out and finding someone to take her place felt just as wrong as what he had to do in the first place.

Shiloh's phone rang, and he looked down to see it was Shya. The smiled that crept across his face let him know that there was no way that he would be able to just give her to the universe, he just couldn't do it. Answering the phone and walking to the back to talk to her, Shiloh had to figure out a way around this.

Ziloh shook his head because he knew that his baby brother was struggling with all of this and in a way, he didn't want it to be her because it would in turn put him in a bad situation with Jalan, but he knew that he couldn't lose his brother because he wanted to be hardheaded.

The knock on the warehouse door drew him from his thoughts. Checking the security camera from his phone, he looked to see it was someone who copped from them on the regular. This nigga from Mooresville. He wasn't sure why he was here, it wasn't his pick-up day. Ziloh grabbed his dick and ran his hand down the front of his shirt and all of the drugs that lined the walls disappeared.

Throwing caution to the wind, Ziloh pulled the door open and there stood a pissed off Channing. Granted, no one knew that Jalan was his girl because the shit he did out in the streets with other women and the fact that he never brought her out in public like that. He still felt disrespected and he planned to tell Ziloh all about it.

"What's up nigga why you looking all pissed off and shit?" Ziloh turned his back to Channing and walked into the warehouse.

Channing's eyes scanned the warehouse that was normally filled with drugs and wondered why it was empty. Nothing was there, not even an ounce of coke.

"I need you to stay away from my girl." Channing didn't waste any time, he wanted the issue out there and corrected so he could go and do some damage control in his home.

"Say what now?" Ziloh turned around slowly, he wanted to make sure that he heard him correctly. He knew good and damn well ain't no grown ass man approaching him about his bitch. There was no way that he was about to have this conversation.

Standing with his feet spread apart and his arms crossed across his chest. He could feel the anger flowing through his veins. Ziloh ran his tongue across the top row of his teeth as his nose flared. He was trying his best to calm down but the fact that this nigga brought that to his place of business wasn't sitting right with him.

"Jalan!" was the only thing that Channing said next and it changed everything about this situation and undoubtedly put Channing's life in danger.

In Ziloh's mind, it was his fault that Jalan was so broken, it was his fault that he didn't get to explore her like he wanted to, and it was his fucking fault that he was gonna have to repair what the fuck he did in order to get to the best parts of her.

"What about her?"

"I need you to stay away from her. We are going through a rough patch right now and I can't fix my shit with you in the way. So as a man I'm asking you to take a step back." Matching Ziloh's demeanor, he too spread his feet and crossed his arms.

This brought humor into the situation for Ziloh. Channing was trying to stand his ground not knowing that if Ziloh wanted to, he could wipe the ground right out from under his feet, literally. Releasing a frustrated chuckle Ziloh shook his head and lowered it, taking a few deep breaths before his eyes fell on Channing again.

"Tell her to come tell me that she doesn't want to see me anymore and I'll back off."

"She doesn't have anything to do with this."

"She has everything to do with this," Ziloh countered causing Channing's chest to puff out.

He didn't know what he expected but he didn't expect to be challenged when it came to his woman. He began to question just how well they knew each other and how long they had been dealing with each other.

"Did you fuck my girl?" Channing couldn't help himself, he had to know if Ziloh was blessed to have invaded her greatness, the greatness that he took for granted as often as he could.

That pulled a full-blown laugh out of Ziloh. He knew that if he wanted to, he could lie to him and fuck his whole world up. He shook the thoughts from his mind and decided to give Channing a lesson in women, one that his fucking father should have taught him.

"Nah I didn't, I could have though." Ziloh tugged on his chin hair. "She wanted the dick and I damn sure wanted to lay her on my bed and spread her legs as far as they can go and drag my tongue up and down her swollen clit right before I fucked the hurt that you caused right out of her." Ziloh paused for theatrics before he continued. Channing hung on to every word. "But I knew that wasn't what she needed, you already treat her like she's nothing but someone to pass the time. Fucking her best friend and shit."

"You don't know a damn thing!"

"Yeah I know more than you think. I bet you don't even know how she likes to sleep. Like how she likes to lay her head on my chest and drape her leg over mine, while her arm wraps around my neck so she knows that I can't move without her knowing." Ziloh shook his head. "I bet you didn't know that her top lip curls slightly when she smiles or that when she laughs, she snorts right before she throws her head back. Or how about the fact that she hates to feel alone which is how you've made her feel the last two years. One night and I've covered more ground than you have your whole relationship."

If it was physically possible, you would be able to see steam coming from Channing's ears. He was so mad that he couldn't form words. Ziloh had done something that he possibly couldn't reverse, he got into her heart.

Channing could feel Jalan slipping from his hands just that quick. Sex he could compete with, but he had treated Jalan so bad that he didn't know if there was a way to cover the space that Ziloh had possibly possessed that quick.

"Just stay away from her."

"I won't do that. Unless she tells me, she doesn't want anything else to do with me then I will continue on my mission to obtain her heart." The sneaky grin that covered Ziloh's face sickened Channing.

What he wanted to do was shoot Ziloh in the head and call it a day, but he knew that he needed to be smart about that. He had never seen him with a team but the fact that they supplied damn near the whole east coast he had to have one. Channing had another idea though.

Turning around and heading to the car so he could get home to talk to Jalan, he picked up his phone. "Detective Price please."

❧ 10 ❧

"What am I gonna do Jalan? I can't do this. My heart won't let me!" Shya cried as her sister sat across from her. The two decided to go to lunch. After Channing left her house, she packed a light bag and decided to go and stay with her sister for a little while. Today they were having a girl's day out.

"I know," Jalan said feeling sad herself about the situation because she knew if anything happened to Shiloh that it would more than likely ruin her chances with Ziloh and she wanted that more than she cared to admit.

After her conversation with Channing she knew that more than ever. Everything that Channing was saying everything that she wanted but it was too late. He had done way too much to her for her to forget about and in such a short amount of time Ziloh had come in and fixed everything that he broke.

"I'm gonna make him hate me, that's what I'll do," Shya's words were lacking confidence. She didn't understand why she had to meet Shiloh now. He was everything that she had ever dreamed about.

He was a thug with a soft side, one that was just for her and she lived for it. She didn't see her life without it. Sacrificing him was out of the question and it was that moment that she knew.

"Why don't you just find someone else Shya, do like I did. Just don't choose the wrong man." A frustrated chuckle left her mouth as she thought about the path she set before herself.

"But I don't want anyone else," Shya whined.

"I know but you have to do what you have to do, I can't lose you Shya and that's what will happen if you don't give your offering back to the universe."

"Jalan I know damn!" Shya yelled and the glasses on the table began to shake, each sister grabbed their glass before anyone noticed.

"Shit girl chill, damn!"

"Well I need you to be my sister and be there for me not lecture me." Shya rolled her eyes and Jalan giggled. Shya threw her a look as if to ask what was funny.

"Spoiled little witch bitch," Jalan said low enough for the two to hear and they shared a laugh. Jalan used to call Shya that when she was younger because she stayed getting Jalan in trouble for not doing what she asked. Being the baby had its perks.

"Seriously, what do I do?"

"I don't know sis, but we gotta figure something out. It's a week till your birthday."

Shya sighed, still trying to figure out how she fell in love in less than a month. She had been spending so much time with Shiloh and she's been in heaven. They had so much in common and she loved how attentive he was and how interested in her that he was. There wasn't anything that she didn't like about him, he was damn near perfect.

"How did he get me that quick?" Shya said more to herself than her sister.

"That dick!" Jalan said louder than Shya wanted her too, the sisters caught a few stares from those closest to them. "That's why the hell you spent, Shiloh done came in and fuck yo ass to love."

"I hate you so much sometimes." Tears were flowing down Shya's face from laughing at her sister so hard. The relationship that the two had was amazing which was why Jalan was pushing Shya so hard to do what she needed to do with the Love Ritual, she couldn't lose her sister for nothing and nobody.

"What about Richard?"

Richard was a guy that Shya dealt with from time to time. It was nothing serious, and nothing that Shya really wanted to pursue other than when she was in the mood to get her pussy ate by a professional because that was the only thing that he could do for her.

"Really bitch?" Shya said between clenched teeth.

"I'm just saying Shya. I'm trying to help the situation."

"Well you're not!" Shya rolled her eyes.

"You need some dick, you should call Shiloh." Jalan tilted her head and Shya tried hard not to smile but it didn't work. A huge grin crept on her face and the two burst out laughing again.

"I got some this morning bitch," Shya giggled like a school girl. She was so smitten with the man that had commanded not only her body but her heart, mind and was working his way into her soul. All in less than a month. "You on the other hand need to get flipped, tossed and bent."

"Ughhh girl I've been trying." Jalan rolled her eyes. "I guess Channing knows Ziloh, he works with him or something, but he stopped by there the other day to confess his love for me and tell Ziloh to back off."

"Girl you lying."

"Bitch I wish, so Ziloh asked me if I was over him and I couldn't answer that because technically we're not even broke up. I just need to have a conversation with Channing, so I can get the closure that I need. But Ziloh said that he wasn't entering my body until he occupied my heart and mind first. He said that the physical part of us would come when everything else lined up."

Shya cupped her hands around her mouth. "Awww that's so sweet."

"Fuck all that, I'm trying to get tossed and flipped as you say. I want that man so bad I felt like knocking him out and taking the dick a few times." Shya laughed but Jalan was so serious.

"You stupid, and it's flipped, tossed and bent, and in that order," Shya joked with her sister.

"Well whatever it is I need the shit and I need it now," Jalan sighed. "But I don't know what's up with Channing, he's been texting me and calling me apologizing. Telling me that he wants to make things right and he'll do whatever he needs to do to do that."

"And?"

Shya was trying her hardest to not judge her sister but the last thing that she needed was for her sister to go running back to that dead-end relationship. Yes, she caused it but Jalan deserved so much more in Shya's eyes. She felt like her sister had already paid her dues for casting that love spell. It was time for her to be happy now.

"Chill, I can't do it. Him and Zeta broke me. I would never be able to look at either of them the same. Speaking of she has been calling me since the day she got arrested." Shya giggled knowing that she was the reason she landed in jail. "But I have nothing to say to her. She and Channing should just go live happily ever after and leave me be. They have my blessing."

"Girl." Shya stood up and started to clap drawing the stares of everyone in the restaurant.

"I'm gonna slap the shit out of you hoe." Jalan shook her head but joined her sister in laughing.

"We should go out tonight. We both got a lot of shit going on and we deserve a night out." Shya just wanted to let her hair down and enjoy a night with her sister and possibly slip in Shiloh's bed tonight.

"Hell yeah, I'm down! But I got to go to my house and get something to wear. God, I hope he's not home." Her eyes rolled in the back of her head.

"I'll go with you, I haven't cooked up a good spell in a minute."

"Oh God, no I'll be fine." Jalan shook her head because she knew that if her sister was thinking like that going into the situation then she would be looking for a reason to do it.

"Nope too late, check please," she told the waiter that was walking by. Jalan prayed that Channing wasn't home, and this would be an in and out situation. In her heart of hearts, she knew that wouldn't be the case. She almost had half the mind to just go buy something but the cute dress that Ziloh bought her weeks ago was calling her name and she desperately wanted to wear it.

CHANNING RUBBED HIS TEMPLE AS HE LISTENED TO ZETA GO ON AND

on about how she was the best option for him and how trying to work things out with Jalan was a mistake. He didn't really care what she was saying because he had already made up his mind that he was proposing to Jalan the minute he laid eyes on her.

He didn't know if it would work or not but right now, he was willing to do anything. She hadn't been home in almost a week. He had followed her once from Shya's house and the two ended up at a mini mansion where they were greeted by Ziloh and his brother Shiloh.

His heart hurt just thinking about what he was possibly doing to her. He didn't even care that she had slept with another man, he was willing to accept that if she would just take him back. This new-found love for her was foreign but it was there, and he couldn't help himself.

What was weird was that he still had feelings for Zeta, but they didn't overpower the ones that were creeping in for Jalan. If you would have asked him a month ago who he thought he was gonna spend the rest of his life with the answer would have been Zeta but now it was completely different. He didn't know if it was an ego thing or what it was, but it was affecting his life right now.

"I'm still trying to figure out what you mean by you don't want to see me anymore?" Zeta's hands were on her thick hips and her lips were poked out showing just how much she hated the words coming out of Channing's mouth.

"Listen, we were just having fun Zeta. I never told you that we would be more than this."

"Yes, the hell you did. You told me that you didn't want to be with her and you saw something with me. What changed?"

"SHE DID!" Channing yelled truthfully. It was something about the thought of Jalan being with someone else that sparked something in him, at least that's what he was telling himself.

"I did what?" Neither of them heard Jalan walk through the door and up the stairs to the bedroom she used to share with Channing. She heard the later part of their argument and to hear Zeta say that Channing made plans to be with her stung a bit, but she knew neither of them were worth her pain.

"Ja—um what—how—listen baby, can we just sit down and talk about this?" Channing tried to explain himself but there was nothing that he could say to make the situation better. This just solidified the decision she made.

"I don't want to listen, all I want is for you to let me be. Let me live my life. The two of you have my blessing." Jalan was over it, however she did want to punch Zeta in the face for being a deceitful bitch and stab Channing in the eye but neither of them were worth the energy.

"I can't do that, I won't see you out living and being happy with Ziloh." The distain that rolled off his tongue from having to speak Ziloh's name was evident and comical to Jalan.

"Why because that would mean that I would actually be happy? You don't think I deserve to be happy, do you?" Her tone was calm and collected, Shya couldn't understand why that was because if it was her, she would literally be a human hurricane. She didn't play when it came to respect and the fact that the two of them were disrespecting her sister, it was killing her not to react.

"You can be happy but with me."

"Channing!" Zeta yelled right before she turned towards her former best friend. She knew once she said what she had to say that she would no longer have a best friend. "Listen, me and Channing been talking for months and then we finally decided to meet up. He told me that y'all were pretty much over anyway."

"But bitch that's your fucking friend, your fucking loyalty was to her. What the fuck you mean he said they were over? That wasn't a fucking green light for yo hoe ass to fuck him!" Shya yelled causing the lights to flicker. Jalan put her hand on her sister's shoulder to calm her down. She could feel the energy surging through her sister, but it wasn't worth the time and effort she was dying to give.

"This has nothing to do with you Shya, you should mind your business."

"Bitch.." Shya took a step towards Zeta but Jalan stepped in front of her so she couldn't get to her.

"She is the only person that gives a fuck about me be sides Ziloh, so yeah it has something to do with her. She's the one that listens to me cry about the betrayal of two people who I thought cared about me enough not fuck me over!" It was Jalan's turn to get upset, no one fucks with her baby sister. "I was wrong though and that was my fuck up!"

"Damn bitch you are mad, I ain't never heard you say fuck that much."

"Shut up Shya," Jalan threw over her shoulder and Shya threw her hands up with a smile on her face. She loves this confidence that Jalan was portraying, she prayed that this was a permanent change and not just because she was mad. "You two deserve each other, you're both disrespectful, disloyal, no good bitches. A match made in fucking heaven."

"Jalan baby I swear I can make it up to you."

"He said that you were just someone to pass the time, that you didn't have the spark that he found in me," Zeta interrupted Channing with a wicked grin on her face.

"This hoe about to make me get real ignorant," Shya said to her sister's back.

"Do you know how many girls he's fucking right now?" Jalan asked Zeta and she turned to look at Channing who's face was stoned, he was caught and didn't have an answer for anything that was about to be thrown at him. Jalan turned toward her sister and whispered.

"Throughout the lies and past deceit,
this man was never really for me.
He crushed my heart and broke my trust,
I deserve to know it all, honesty's a must."

Jalan tucked her hair behind her left ear and waited for Channing to reveal his truth.

"I did somethings that I'm not proud of and I feel like you should know everything," he started out as he revealed every woman he's cheated on Jalan with, what was more shocking was that he revealed that he was now sleeping with two other women outside of Zeta. That really pissed Zeta off because she thought that Channing was it for her and that she had something on Jalan.

"You have fun with that you funky mouth bitch." Shya flipped Zeta off and took off after her sister while Zeta and Channing engaged in a very heated conversation. "We'll just use magic to get all your shit out of there when he goes to sleep or when he's not there."

"Yeah, but I need the dress that Ziloh bought me." Jalan remembered her reasoning for coming there in the first place. She ran back up in the room and went to the closet to grab the bag. When Channing stopped her.

"Marry me!"

"What?" Jalan stopped in her tracks and refused to turn around and look at him. "What did you just say?"

"Marry me, I know I've done some dumb shit, but I swear I'm done with all of that. Everything is out on the table now, all you have to do is forgive me and we'll be all good."

An angry chuckle left Jalan's lips as she turned around slowly. "You have got to be out of your rabbit ass mind. I would never marry you, you've hurt me so bad and I know it was my fault, but I'll never see you in that light again. Your best bet is to live happily ever after with that hoe." She pointed at Zeta who had joined them in the closet. Jalan bent down and grabbed the bag she was looking for. When she stood up, she walked in Zeta's direction. "And you bitch, I hope he fucks you over so bad you lose yourself in his bullshit way worse than I ever did." Jalan cocked back and hit Zeta right in the mouth causing her to go crashing to the floor. "You deserved more than that, but I'mma let you live hoe."

With that Jalan walked out of the house and out of Channing's life. She was excited to find out what life had in store for her.

❦ II ❧

"I'm telling you what to do bruh, find another bitch, fuck her, make the hoe fall in love and then live happily ever after with Shya. The shit ain't that hard."

"Nigga you just know if something happens to Shya, Jalan ain't gone be fucking with you no more."

"You fucking right and I'm feeling shorty, I planned on giving her the dick real soon." Ziloh laughed and grabbed his dick causing a shipment of dope to appear on the table beside where he was standing. "You ain't about to fuck that shit up for me."

The two brothers joined in on a laugh, spirits were light even though the fact that Shiloh's birthday was right around the corner and he knew what was at stake. He tried not to think about it, but it was something that he couldn't get past.

One thing he did know was that Shya was gonna be a part of his life, for as long as he was alive. Sacrificing her was not something that he was willing to do, so finding someone to take her place may just have to suffice.

The ritual states that the person had to love you not that you had to love them. Shiloh was starting to see his brother's point, even though his dick had grown accustomed to Shya he may have to spread some love to get his forever.

Knock! Knock! Knock! Someone knocking on the warehouse door pulled Shiloh from his thoughts, before he could pull out his phone Ziloh was already looking to see who at the door.

"The fuck the police want?" he said more to himself. Shiloh grabbed his dick and brushed his shirt and all the drugs disappeared and the room was clear outside of the couch and the tv in the corner. "The kitchen," Ziloh said before he grabbed himself to make sure everything was cleared.

Opening the door, a detective in plain clothes and two uniformed officers walked into the building like they belonged there. Shiloh sent a text to his father and to their lawyer for them to get there right away. Neither of the brother said anything they just stood back and watched them do whatever it was they were doing.

"Where are the drugs?" the detective in plain clothes finally asked. Shiloh looked down at his phone and it was a text from his father saying that someone by the name of Channing called in the tip. That drew a chuckle from Shiloh who tilted the phone towards his brother.

"Where's the fucking warrant?" Ziloh asked now clearly pissed that this was some bullshit ass get back from Channing who had just signed his death certificate. "I just want you to know you wasted your fucking time, Detective ..." Ziloh held his hand out for the detective to answer him.

"Price but who I am is neither here nor there. Where are the drugs? I know they're here! Who tipped you off?"

"Nigga ain't nobody tipped nobody off. Ain't shit here, you got played," Shiloh laughed in Detective Price's face, whose bright yellow skin had taken on a red color.

"Channing is pissed that I took his girl, he's the one who told you that shit ain't he?" Ziloh raised a brow and waited for an answer from Detective Price that he was never gonna get.

"Let's go," he told the officers. "We'll be back!"

"Next time bring a warrant, you'll be hearing from my lawyer," Shiloh said but Ziloh already knew how he was gonna get back at the officers. He grabbed his dick and narrowed his eyes and watched as

Detective Price stumbled as he got to the door. A smile crept on Ziloh's face as he waved at a now drunk Detective Price.

"The fuck you just do?" Shiloh laughed once they were alone.

"That nigga going back to work smelling like he just drank a pint of buck and when they make his ass blow, he gone blow double the legal limit," Ziloh doubled over laughing. He thought that was the funniest thing in the world, he loved his magical abilities.

"You a fool for that one."

"Fuck that nigga and after we handle this business at Onyx tonight I'mma knock that nigga off. Jalan won't even have to worry about him anymore."

"Ole plotting as nigga, let's fucking go. Let me text pops and tell him we good. He gone cuss yo ass out when he finds out this over some pussy."

"Yo don't say that shit again. You know it ain't even like that," Ziloh's voice held so much power that Shiloh's initial comeback got caught in his throat and all he could do was nod his head and throw his hands up. "What if I said Shya was just pussy." He narrowed his eyes.

"Muthafucka," it was Shiloh's turn to get pissed.

"See nigga, now come the fuck on we got shit to do," Ziloh said with humor in his tone. Shiloh was looking at him like he wanted to fight him and if he wasn't his brother he probably would have.

"Damn," Shiloh hissed as the stripper in his lap did her best tricks trying to get every dime that he had in his pocket. Him and Ziloh had handled the business that they had to handle, and he had gotten drunk so that he could allow himself to open up to someone else.

The shit was harder than he thought it was gonna be, the more he talked to different women the more guilty he felt and the more he drank. Now he was tore up and reason was out the window, he was on a mission and he wasn't stopping until he did what it was he needed to do to keep his relationship with Shya.

"Damn daddy, I think I need to take you home," the girl whispered in his ear.

"Shit play ya cards right and you might just be able to do that," he slurred and grabbed her by the neck and bent her back over so that her ass was up and there was a nice arch in her back. Shya's face flashed in his mind and his hard dick went limp in a matter of seconds.

The stripper turned around with a frown on her face and Shiloh shrugged. He didn't want to tell her that the woman that had his heart had flashed through his mind and any chance of him doing what he needed to do was out the window.

"Maybe if you go freshen up and come back we'll be good." The shocked expression on the stripper's face caused Ziloh to laugh because Shiloh said it loud enough for the people in his section to hear it.

"Damn!" the stripper said clearly pissed off. Shiloh grabbed her arm and handed her a hundred-dollar bill and winked at her and that brightened her spirits. Shaz had been looking for a nigga to take her out of the strip club and when she saw Shiloh and his brother walk in, she knew they had money. "Alright baby, I'll be back."

Shiloh watched as the stripper walked out of the section and down to the locker room. "What the fuck nigga?" Ziloh shoved his arm as he tapped the stripper that was on his lap to dismiss her. "You need to join your friend in the back." The stripper held out her hand and waited for Ziloh to drop a hundred in it and he laughed in her face. "Yo I ain't my brother, I ain't about to lace yo ass, get the fuck out of my face."

The stripper smacked her lips and walked off with an attitude, causing the brothers to laugh. Ziloh shook his head at his brother, he knew he was fucked up and that was the only way that he could do what he needed to do. He felt for his brother because he could relate to him about how he felt for Shya because he felt the same thing about Jalan.

That was the worst part of witchery, you were blessed with the powers, but you had to give the ultimate sacrifice to keep them. The universe wanted what they gave ten times fold. Shit was crazy, but it was worth it in the end.

"Damn I thought about Shya and my dick went down so got damn fast. Like what the fuck?" Shiloh grabbed himself and shook his head. He stood up and walked over to the rail that looked down on the club.

"It's gone work out bruh, we gone make sure you get your girl."

Shiloh just nodded and lowered his head. He felt a small pair of hands on his back and looked over his shoulder and it was the stripper. Shorty was bad as fuck. Skin the color of toasted almonds, light gray eyes, and she had the body of a video vixen. He could easily fuck her on any other day but since Shya had walked into his life he didn't see women like he normally did and for some reason his ass was sobering up quick as hell.

"I need a fucking drink," Shiloh said to himself.

"Aye baby, wanna meet me in the VIP room in the back?" Shaz was about to pull out all the stops and Shiloh didn't know what he was about to walk in to.

"Let's go." Shiloh was about to try one more time to get this right. "Aye bruh grab me a drink, I'm going to the VIP with shorty."

Ziloh looked from the stripper to his brother and then back to her before he nodded his head. "I got you bruh."

Meanwhile across the room, Shya was watching all of this unfold and to say she was pissed would have been an understatement. She had half the mind to pull a Carrie and kill everybody in this club, but she was trying her best to calm down.

"Why in the hell did we come to a strip club again?" Jalan complained for the hundredth time since the two had walked in the building. She was oblivious to the chaos about to unfold because she was too busy snarling her nose up at the naked women walking around.

Jalan wasn't used to coming here but Shya on the other hand thought that it was fun to come and watch the women dance. It was entertaining and educational even to her. Her attention however wasn't on the beautiful women but on the fact that the man that she was feeling was about to take a bitch in the back to be alone. That shit didn't sit right with her.

Following them with her eyes she watched them and exactly which room they went in. "Hey, stand right here, I'm gonna see if my friend is working tonight," she lied to her sister because she didn't need her stopping her.

"I just wanna dance for you," Shaz sang over the music as *Dance for You by Keri Hilson* played through the speakers. Shaz sensually moved her body as she grabbed a handful of her breast as she moved to the beat of the song. Pulling her breast out of the bra, her hips found the beat and moved by themselves as her nipples found her mouth and she gently sucked.

"Got damn," Shiloh pulled his bottom lip into his teeth as he watched Shaz dance for him. The way she was looking at him had him in some sort of trance. His dick slowly rose to it's half potential. "Shit!" he hissed.

"That's it baby," Shaz said as she turned around and bent all of the way over giving him the perfect shot of her freshly waxed pussy. "Look how wet it is for you." She slid her finger over the string of the thong and began to play with herself.

Shya was fuming, her hands shook violently as she sat and thought about the things that she wanted to do to the both of the them. She couldn't believe what she was witnessing right now. The things she told him she had never told anyone, she thought they really connected. She shook her head. He wasn't worth saving after all.

> *"Magic do's and magic don'ts,*
> *right is right and wrong is wrong.*
> *I was willing to give you all of me,*
> *but to you I'm just a piece.*
> *Since you were willing to break my heart,*
> *have fun enjoying her funky farts."*

Shya tucked her hair behind her right ear and watched as Shiloh's face went from one of pure pleasure to one of pure disgust. She could hear the vicious farts coming from the stripper and when the smell hit her, she looked at Shiloh and his eyes were trained on her. Turning to leave she ran right into Ziloh who was looking at her all weird. She hadn't even noticed him so close. She was too busy trying to exert revenge that she didn't check her surroundings.

Had he seen her? She didn't have time to wait around and see. She ran passed him and out to find her sister. "Where the hell have you been?" Jalan asked as soon as she saw her sister. "Did you know that Ziloh was here?"

"We have to go now!" She pulled her sisters arm and Jalan could see the alarm in her face and she knew that whatever had happened it was bad and instead of asking a bunch of questions she just left with her sister, but you better believe she would be getting an answer for her craziness as soon as they got to the house.

Ziloh followed the girls with his eyes trying to figure out if he really just saw what he thought he seen. He could have sworn that he saw Shya doing magic, he heard the spell and then she tucked her hair behind her ear and then the atmosphere in the room changed drastically.

"What the fuck is that smell?" Ziloh asked when he entered the room.

"This nasty bitch won't stop farting." Shiloh's face was scrunched up. "Was that Shya I just saw?"

"Yeah and we need to go."

"Wait, not yet. We didn't finish our dance." Shaz grabbed her stomach. It was normal for her to let a small fart slip every now and then when she danced, hell she couldn't help it, but it felt like she was full of air. Her stomach cramped but she still wanted to shoot her shot.

"Nah, I'm good love." Shiloh threw his hand up and headed in the direction of his brother.

"Got damn bitch what you eat?" Ziloh snarled up once again before he took off in the direction of his brother.

The two walked outside and headed to the car. The smell of Shaz still resonated in the air as the two were trying to get as far away from it as they possibly could. Ziloh was still trying to piece together what the fuck he just saw.

"I saw something that fucked me up a little bit," Ziloh said climbing in the car.

"What?"

"So, when ol' girl was dancing with you, everything was good and then all of a sudden, she started that farting shit right? It was sudden right?"

"Yeah, a nigga was getting right and everything, she was playing in her pussy and for once my dick was hard and I actually thought that I could do this. Then she started that nasty shit."

"It was Shya."

"What was Shya? The fuck you talking about Ziloh? Yo ass been drinking and shit?"

"Nigga I know what the fuck I heard and saw. She was looking in that room when I was bringing your drink. She said some shit about you breaking her heart or some shit. I know that shit rhymed, I remember moms used to do that rhyming shit and then crazy shit happened. All I know is the minute she tucked her hair behind her ear the whole atmosphere of the room changed. Your face went from fuck yeah to fuck you, nigga."

"You saying she a witch?"

"Nigga I think so."

"Ain't this a fucking bitch? So, she been lying and hiding shit from me." Shiloh began to pace the parking lot. He was getting pissed off because the street lights were starting to flicker. "That's why when we fuck we break shit."

"Nigga shut the fuck up." Ziloh waved his brother off. He felt like he was making a mockery of it now. He was serious, this shit was fucking crazy. What were the fucking odds?

"No nigga, I'm serious. The first time we fucked we came together, and the lights flickered and shit and then burst, the dresser shook and then the bed broke. Our energy together was too high. Hell, I thought I just came that hard." Shiloh laughed and shook his head. "No wonder her ass didn't freak out. We just laughed it off and kept it moving."

"I knew it was sometign about them that I couldn't put my finger on. The damn energy was too fucking high when we were together." Ziloh looked down and then back up at Shiloh like a light bulb went off in his head. "We need to find them because if Shya's a witch then..."

"Jalan is too," Shiloh finished his brothers' sentence and they jumped in the car and pulled out. Shit just got real and they weren't sure how it was all gonna unfold.

❦ 12 ❦

rash! A glass plate floated out of the cabinet and hit the wall. Jalan hated when Shya got excited or mad because she couldn't control her ability to move things with her mind and things could get crazy fast. Shya hadn't quite gotta grip with that power yet.

"Calm down Shya," Jalan attempted to get her sister to tell her what happened so she could begin to fix the problem. She couldn't fix it if she didn't know what it was.

"Don't tell me to calm down Jalan!" she yelled. The lights flickered, and the cabinets began to open and shut. "You didn't see what I saw!"

The neighbors were sure to call the police at any minute if she didn't calm down. It had happened before, so it was sure to happen again. Shya had never felt the way she felt right now, it was like someone was taking her heart and ripping it out of her chest and all she wanted to do was crawl in a hole and die but not before she took a few people with her.

"What did you see?" Jalan gave her sister a sympathetic look, she knew she was hurting, she could feel it to a degree. Her energy was off, and she just wanted to make everything better.

"He was in that room with some funky ass bitch, she was playing in her used pussy while he sat there and bit his lip like he was excited. I could see his dick print poking through his pants. What the fuck was he doing?" The tears that found their way down her eyes proved that she was pissed beyond words and nothing that Jalan could say would help the hurt that she felt.

There was only one person that could ease that pain and he was on the other side of the door watching shit flying across the room and lights flickering on and off like before. He looked at his brother before his head fell in his hands.

Shiloh couldn't believe that this was happening right now. The girl that he was in love with was a witch just like he was. He didn't know how that worked in the world of witchery, but he had a feeling that it wouldn't work out too well for the two of them. You couldn't sacrifice another witch, so he was left without a gift to the universe.

"What the fuck man?" Shiloh said.

Ziloh on the other hand found it funny, she seemed to be one powerful ass witch and it was sexy in his eyes. He wanted to see what Jalan had to offer. At first, he was pissed at her for not telling him but then it hit him, he was hiding shit from her too.

"I hope her funky ass farts burned his fucking nose hairs!" she yelled, and the front door flew open on its own and Shiloh stood face to face with a tear strained Shya. He felt like shit when all he was trying to do was save her life and have her in the same breath. He didn't intentionally mean to hurt her, and if he could take it back, he would. "What the fuck are you doing here?" her once light brown eyes had taken on a dark gray color and her hair was wet like she had been in a swimming pool, but she was still sexy nonetheless.

Raising her hand, she swiped it in the air and the door went full force in the direction of the brothers but Ziloh put his hand up to stop it and Jalan gasped. Shya swiped the air again and Ziloh held his hand where it was and the two stood there in a stand off.

"Oh, you have got to be shitting me!" Jalan said taking Shya's attention for just a second giving Ziloh's powers a chance to one up Shya's. Once the door was opened the brother's stepped in the house and shut the door behind them.

"So, when were you going to tell me?" Shiloh stood in front of Shya with his hands tucked deep in his pockets. His smooth dark skin and athletic build tugged at Shya's heart, but she refused to give in to him.

"When the fuck were you going to tell me that you like funky ass strippers?" Shya yelled causing the china cabinet to fly open. Jalan touched her shoulder and she looked down at her sister's hand before she met her stare.

"Yo that shit was foul, I'm still smelling that bitch's ass," Ziloh pointed at Shya and she glared at him before a plate came whirling at his head. "How the fuck you do that without pointing or anything?"

Ziloh wasn't making light out of the situation, he was genuinely interested in how their powers worked. They seemed so different from Warlocks and he wanted to know. Shya growled before she left the kitchen where they were standing making everything in her path shake or fall over.

She was on the brink of getting her full powers, so her powers were a little shaky and less accurate now. When she was mad or excited things broke, moved or shattered, if she thought it, it happened and that was scaring her a bit. She didn't know her strengths and right now wasn't the time for her to be trying to figure it out especially with her being so mad.

"Don't walk away from me!" Shiloh followed behind her.

"Shiloh now is not the time for you to talk to her, maybe later when she calms down." Jalan could feel her sister's energy was high and things could get really bad if they didn't back off.

"You come here for a second." Ziloh pulled Jalan in his direction. He had a few questions for her. How in the hell was she a witch and he not know? He felt like he should have felt her energy or something. "What the hell Jalan?"

"Ohhhhh, don't you what the hell me." She pointed at him as she looked in her sister's direction who was in a serious stare down with Shiloh. "You didn't tell me either Ziloh, I can't believe you're a witch!"

"I'm not a got damn witch, witches are bitches." Jalan reached up and slapped the hell out of the back of his head and he grabbed it and laughed. "I didn't mean it like that."

"But that's what you said."

"Look I don't have time for this, I have to make sure that my sister don't kill you brother. She's pissed at him."

"She can't kill him, he's in his transition stage. That's when a warlock is his most powerful so if anything, we should worry about her," Ziloh told Jalan and she scoffed, she couldn't believe that the two of them were in the same boat. That must have been why he was with the stripper looking for someone to take her place. Jalan's eyes stretched wide.

"Shya is in her transition too." They both looked in the room right before they heard a loud boom. The two took off in the direction of Shy's room and walked in to find the two of them on opposite sides of the room against the wall. "Shya he was trying to find someone to replace you in the Love Ritual, he couldn't sacrifice you."

Jalan said to her sister and Shya looked over to where Shiloh was trying to pick himself up off the floor. He shook his head and glared at Shya who now had a small smile.

"You love me?" she asked above a whisper.

"Are you serious right now? Your ass just tried to fucking kill me, and you want to know if I love you? The hell Shya?" Shiloh didn't know what to think right now, a part of him liked the fact that she was a witch because he wouldn't have to hide who he was but the other side of him was worried that small fact just made the situation worse.

"I thought you were cheating on me with a nasty ass stripper."

"No, I needed her to fall in love with me, so I could give her to the universe and live my life with the woman who owns my heart. Even if she's fucking crazy." Shiloh watched as Shya's crazy looking eyes went back to their beautiful honey color. "Wait, so what the fuck were you gonna do because if I'm in my transition and we're the same age with the same birthday then you had to give up a sacrifice too. Who the fuck was gone be your sacrifice?"

Shya looked at Shiloh who's mouth was tight, and his demeanor had become cold. In his mind the only person that she could have sacrificed was him. What he didn't know that Shya had made up her mind that she would sacrifice herself because she couldn't see life without him.

"Before I saw you with that stripper," she rolled her eyes and he opened his mouth to say something, but she held up her hand, "I know now but still." Jalan chuckled because Shiloh didn't know what he was getting into, but it was his problem and not hers. "I didn't see my life without you so if I had to choose who got to live it would have been you." A lone tear fell from her eyes as Shiloh made his way over to her and wrapped her in his arms.

"You were going to sacrifice yourself for me?" She nodded her head yeah. Jalan sat in the corner and cried because she didn't know that her sister felt that way about Shiloh and she damn sure didn't talk to her about that decision. That conversation was definitely gonna happen with them and soon. "Why would you do that?"

"Because my heart wouldn't allow me not to," her words were honest and pure, you didn't need magic to see that.

"Would you sacrifice yourself for me?" Ziloh asked Jalan who was watching on with tears streaming down her face.

"I don't know how good the dick is, so I can't say," she said causing the room to erupt in laughter.

"I got that covered," he said grabbing her hand.

"There is one good thing that comes out of this," Jalan said gaining everyone's attention. "You can't sacrifice another witch and y'all fell in love with each other. Only downside of that is you have to get permission from the head of your family. Shya I don't know how that's gonna work for you but there's your out." Jalan smiled at her sister.

Shya groaned because she knew how her mother felt about the Love Ritual. She felt that it was our gift to the universe and it blesses our family. In her mind, it was the reason their family bloodline had been strong for the last three centuries.

"Good luck with that shit Shiloh."

"Milo ain't want no smoke," Shiloh said referring to his father. He knew that his father took his witchery seriously, so he didn't know how that was gonna go but he would take that there was a sliver of hope over the possibility of losing Shya.

"Bet," Ziloh said pulling Jalan out of the room where Shya was still in Shiloh's arms. The two sat in silence for what felt like forever.

"Ever get the feeling that everything is gonna be okay?" Shiloh looked down at Shya and a slow smile appeared on his face.

"I get that every time I'm in your arms," Shya said.

"Don't be trying all that sweet shit now, yo ass was like a got damn hurricane earlier. Like what the hell?"

"I thought you broke my heart, I don't take to kindly too that."

"I love you witch."

"I love you too witch nigga," she laughed at her own corny joke.

Shiloh crashed his lips into her and the two spent the rest of the night showing the other how they felt. Neither knew what the outcome of the situation would be, so they made sure to make tonight a night to remember.

On the other side of the house, Ziloh and Jalan wasted no time ripping each other's clothes off. Ziloh was in the push up position debating whether to invade her walls or not. Something was bothering him, and he needed to know the answer to the question that was plaguing his mind.

"I'm gonna kill your ex," he said calmly as if he was saying he was gonna smash a bug or something. Jalan thought about the words that were coming out of his mouth, and the fact that they didn't phase her she knew that her feelings for Channing were out of her system.

"Okay, that's fine now can you shut the hell up and fuck the shit out of me already?" She threw her head on the pillow causing Ziloh to laugh.

"You can't rush greatness," he laughed again and eased into her. She gave a lot of pushback as he worked his hips in a circle making his way into her. "You gotta relax and let me in," he leaned down and whispered in her ear. "I thought you wanted me to fuck you? Open up," he teased.

"The shit hurts!" she yelled at him.

"Only for a second." He nibbled on her earlobe taking her mind off the pain as he pushed himself in in one thrust. "Oh fuck!" he said as she clamped her pussy around his dick.

"Ummmm sssss!"

"This is mine, you're mine. No matter what." He leaned up so the two were looking at each other. "Do you hear me?"

"No matter what." She tucked her lip between her teeth as she wound her hips from under him. Jalan wanted to be fucked, flipped, tossed and bent, and all Ziloh was trying to do was talk. He shook his head at her eagerness but succumbed to her request.

Ziloh worked her body over like never before. He showed her what she had been missing in her life and she enjoyed every minute of it.

❧ 13 ❧

"**H**appy birthday baby," Shya said as she placed her hands on Shiloh's chest and used it for leverage as she bounced her ass up and down on his dick. She was giving him a dose of the best birthday sex that she could give.

"Shit happy birthday to you!" He bit down on his bottom lip. The two had been going at it for over an hour and they were about to be late for their ceremonies. "You gone make me nut."

"Come on baby, cum with me," she said and bounced harder. Her head went back, and her mouth fell open. She was in pure bliss. This was by far the best birthday she ever had.

"Damn baby ride that shit!" Shiloh looked down, enjoying the way the sweat rolled down her sexy stomach and how the light hit her skin just right giving it a magical glow. It was enough to bring Shiloh where he needed to be.

"I'm about to cum baby, shit this feels so got damn good! Fuck I love you!"

"Shit I love you too!" Shiloh's stomach got tight as he shot his load in her womb. As normal, the lights flickered, and the dresser shook. They both exploded and Shya found her head on Shiloh's chest where she attempted to get herself together. "I wonder what our kids will be like?" Shiloh said.

"Crazy as fuck!" Shya said and the two laughed. They both knew that it was true though. The both of them had quick tempers and their attitudes weren't the best, combine the two and you have something crazy. "If we don't get to this ceremony neither one of us will live long enough to find out."

Shya climbed off of Shiloh and headed to the shower to clean off. Shiloh laid in the bed and just thought about how good the universe had been to him lately. Not only did he meet the woman of his dreams, but she turned out to be a witch. And what makes it even better is that they found a way around the Love Ritual. After meeting with their family, they learned that if you fall in love with a witch and the feelings are mutual then you don't have to sacrifice that love, but you still had to give back to the universe.

The catch was, you had to sacrifice someone who has hurt someone you love. Good thing for Shya and Shiloh that was easy. Shya choose to sacrifice Zeta for the disrespect and disloyalty that she showed her sister and Shiloh chose Channing for initially trying to get them put in jail even though it back fired on him.

Tonight, they had to give their gifts to the universe. They were already late, but Shiloh just couldn't allow midnight to roll around without him being inside the woman he loves for their birthday. The way he saw it, they had fought hard to get the universe to see things their way, so she could wait a few minutes for them to make their own traditions.

Stepping into Razza, Jalan and Shya's mom's basement the atmosphere was calm, but you could feel the fear radiating off of Channing and Zeta who were laying side by side in the middle of the floor. Jalan had given them both a potion that allowed them to see and feel but not able to move.

The two were dressed in all white robes, the hood's covered their heads. Candles surrounded the dark room. Kneeling in front of the sacrificial offerings Shya and Shiloh looked at each other and smiled.

Never in a million years did the other think that they would have found someone who shares the same gifts as them. It made everything with them that much better. The energy in the room was high and everyone could feel it, even Channing and Zeta.

"Can I say something." Jalan burst through the doors of the basement drawing a hateful look from her mother. Ziloh was right behind her and received the same look. "I'm sorry mom I just need to do this, for me." she gave her mother a sympathetic look and her mother returned it.

Nothing about this ceremony was traditional so what would it hurt for Jalan to get closure for her past mistake. Walking over to where Channing was laying with fear pooling around his eyes, a lone tear fell and for a second Jalan felt sorry for him. All that ended the minute her sister's eyes met hers.

She would give anything for her sister, especially a man who didn't give a damn about her. Channing didn't know what was going on, all he knew was that Jalan called him to talk and he invited her over to the house and that was the last thing he remembered. Now he lay on a cold basement floor unable to move and speak.

The candles that surrounded him scared the shit out of him and every time he looked at Zeta, he cursed her because he felt that she was the reason they were in this mess. If she had never come on to him then Jalan would have never known what he had been up to and everything would be fine.

"My karma was having to deal with all of your shit, when I cast that spell for you to love me I made the biggest mistake of my life. You're Karma will be spending eternity far off in the universe with the bitch you wanted."

Confusion replaced the fear in Channing's eyes, he couldn't put together the words that Jalan were speaking. What did she mean, spells and universe, she wasn't making sense?

"Ohhh yeah, we some Hood Witches!" Shya said with a huge smile on her face.

Channing's eyes stretched wide and Zeta's eyes were full of tears, she was silently pleading for Jalan to forgive her. Had she known what she was getting into she would have stayed away from Channing. Trying to cry out for the thousandth time to no avail caused her to shut her eyes tightly and send a prayer up to God to have mercy on her soul.

"Don't pray now bitch." Jalan said before she shook her head and took her place back beside Ziloh who wrapped his arms around her and squeezed. Surprisingly, she wasn't bothered by what was going on, she knew that it had to happen, and she also knew that she had an amazing man behind her.

Grabbing the bottle of potion that Jalan had prepared, Razza slowly poured the potion the length of Zeta. Milo, Shiloh and Ziloh's father, performed the same action to Channing. Smoke started to fill the room while the family began to chant...

Love is pure, love is true
I give this sacrifice unto you

The more they chanted the more smoke filled the room, and the candles began to flicker. All of a sudden a strong gust of wind blew through the room, taking out all of the candles. The chanting slowly stopped and a bright light filled the room right before it fell dark again.

A few moments passed before someone flicked the light switch, everyone looked around the room. The space that once was occupied by Channing and Zeta was empty, the shape of a heart was burned in the floor where they once were.

"Is it over?" Shya looked around and then to Shiloh.

"It's over." He smiled and pulled her into his arms. The universe was on their side and they were in complete and utter bliss.

"I SEE YOU TWO JUST AIN'T GONE DO RIGHT HUH?" RAZZA, SHYA AND Jalan's mother said after the ceremony was complete and the couples had sat down to eat the feast prepared by Razza and Cheyene, Shiloh and Ziloh's mom.

"We're trying," Shya said with a sneaky smile on her face.

"Trying my got damn ass," Milo, the brothers' father said. Ziloh definitely got his mouth from his father. Everyone laughed. "But I'm glad y'all found each other."

"Shit me too pops," Shiloh said crashing his lips into Shya, who accepted happily.

"I'm just happy to know that our blood line will become stronger and live on for many years to come," Razza said. She knew that the Rage family bloodline was just as strong and as the Hood so when the girls came to her about the falling for the Rage brothers she didn't hesitate, but either way they had to give a gift to the universe.

Ziloh and Jalan had been holed up at Ziloh's house since the first night they had sex. Only coming out to be there for their siblings. The two had explored each other so much there wasn't a spot on the other's body that they didn't know about.

"Well I just want to say whatever energy brought y'all two together, I appreciate it cause y'all helped this to happen," Ziloh said. "A nigga happy as hell."

"Flipped, tossed and bent." Jalan held up her drink and Shya toasted with her and the four laughed while their parents looked on trying to figure out what the hell they were talking about.

"Life never felt so good," Shiloh spoke up.

"Hey, who said you can't find love with some Hood Witches?" Shyla smiled right before she attacked Shiloh's lips.

The End!

ALSO BY NIKKI BROWN

Messiah and Reign 1-3

I Won't Play A Fool For You (Messiah and Reign spinoff)

My Love And His Loyalty 1-3

I Deserve your love 1-3

Bury My Heart 1-2

Beautiful Mistake 1-3

Beautiful Revenge

Riding Hard For A Thug 1-3

You're The Cure To The Pain He Caused

Key To The Heart Of A Boss 1-3

I Got Love For A Carolina Hustla 1-3

A Hood Love Like No Other 1-2

Vexed: The Streets Never Loved Me 1-2

Hood Witches

CPSIA information can be obtained
at www.ICGtesting.com
Printed in the USA
LVHW031725081218
599771LV00001B/18/P